To my Guardian a_ _

MW01107960

SUMMARY

Amy Lafitte spent thirteen years in an Orphanage, on a private island, in the Irish Sea between Scotland and Ireland. She was rescued at the age of eighteen by her Aunt Lily and brought to the family home in the New Orleans French Quarter. When she was safe at home she found out that her Mom and Dad had survived the cruise ship tragedy that brought her to the Orphanage at the age of five. She learned that she had a Granny, who was a three hundred year old witch, and a Grandfather who was the real pirate Jean Lafitte, an immortal.

Amy met Jimmy O'Brien, a Leprechaun, who was neither short nor mean but four feet tall and had a sense of humor to match her own.

Amy and Jimmy start the French Quarter Detective Agency. Their first clients are looking for their nephew, Bugs Robichaux, who disappeared over a year ago. Bugs inherited Castle Island in the middle of the Bermuda Triangle, off Key West, and his Aunts inherited a pirate treasure map. Since the map showed the pirate treasure was somewhere on the island Bugs agreed to find the treasure and maybe sell the island.

To his amazement Bugs sells the island to the current tenants for two million dollars cash. He leaves with a suitcase full of money heading for Key West to deposit the money in a bank before returning to find the treasure.

In a rental boat, on the way to Key West, Bugs strangely falls asleep and wakes up in a dungeon. The cash is missing. Had he been kidnapped by pirates?

Amy and Jimmy fly to Miami. On the plane Amy meets Harry Morgan, a love interest, who helps her in her quest to find Bugs.

There's a surprise at the end and it's even more surprising than even Amy can imagine and Amy has a great imagination!

"In loving memory of Lynne Marie Rivet."

Amy and the French Quarter Detective Agency

CASE #1: The Missing Pirate Treasure Map

Judy Garwood

Amy and the French Quarter Detective Agency

CASE #1: The Missing Pirate Treasure Map

Copyright © 2015 by Judy Garwood

ISBN-13: 978-1547200726

Cover Design and Illustration by Ray Taix

My thanks to my dear friends Beth, Ray and Linda for being my Guardian Angels and to Ray Taix for the incredible art work on the front and back covers and also the hand drawings on my books. Ray Taix is a creative artist and I'm grateful to call him my friend.

"I'm never bored when I have a book in my hand."

- Judy Garwood

Table of Contents

PROLOGUE

The first thought Bugs Robichaux had, when he regained consciousness, was that if he could feel the cold stone floor he was laying on, then he wasn't dead. Looking around he didn't know whether to be happy he was still alive or panicked because he was trapped in a large dark cave. Waves of sea water lapped gently at a small sandy beach. Where he expected to see stars and sky was the soaring ceiling of the frigid cave, home to spiders. Huge hairy spiders. He hated spiders.

Bugs carefully stood up and looked around. The cave was lit by ceiling lights. Against the wall were a lot of boxes labeled MRE's known in the military as Meals Ready to Eat. There was enough food to last for a long time. Utility shelves lined the walls with five gallon plastic containers of water. Bugs stopped counting after one hundred. At least he wouldn't run out of food or water.

Almost giddy with joy he spotted a radio, a clock and a TV. There was also a queen size bed, an end table with a lamp and two bookcases that held books and notebooks. There was even an old fashioned typewriter. He found writing pens, aspirin and vitamins in the top drawer of the end table. In the far corner there was a proper bathroom with a toilet, sink and shower. Bugs guessed the waste water must be connected to a septic system.

It all came rushing back to him. He had inherited Castle Island off Key West, Florida. Auntie Lynne and Auntie Gayle, who had been like mothers to him when at a young age his Mom and Dad died, inherited a pirate treasure map that described a chest with gold and jewels somewhere on the island. He promised his aunts he'd find the treasure for them and decide what he would do with the Island. He immediately set out for Key West. It was a complete surprise to find a Gothic Castle on the Island, with long standing tenants, who were eager to purchase the Castle they called Ravensclaw. After asking what he thought to be an incredible price they agreed and bought the Castle, the Island and the fifty private acres for two million dollars in cash. After being welcomed to stay as long as he wanted at Ravensclaw Bugs decided to take the large leather luggage, holding the cash, to Key West. After that was safely deposited in the bank he would return to search for the pirate treasure before returning home to New Orleans. He wisely decided not to mention the treasure to the new buyers of Ravensclaw. He had sold them the Castle, not the treasure hidden somewhere on the Island. He hid the map in his room at Ravensclaw.

The last thing he remembered was heading his rented speedboat towards Key West. He checked his charts and was glad he'd gotten an early start. Calm seas, clear skies, and no rain in sight meant he would be in Key West shortly. Then for no reason he could figure out he nodded his head and went to sleep. He vaguely remembered hearing an explosion. Then everything went black as a night, without the moon's glow.

He was grateful he was still alive but the leather bag holding his two million dollars in cash was missing and he was alone in a cave dungeon. Had he been kidnapped by pirates?

CHAPTER ONE

Amy and Jimmy Start a Detective Agency

The day after Mardi Gras, in the French Quarter, is almost as noisy as the night before only it's not serious party goers making all the noise, it's heavy duty cleaning trucks.

Just before dawn they sweep through the deserted streets pushing broken Hurricane glasses, torn plastic beer cups, smashed Mardi Gras beads and containers of to-go Red Beans and Rice, Jambalaya, Gumbo and broken sticks that once held grilled alligator tail meat.

This molten, broken mixture is swept to the curbs and then sucked into giant holding tanks that are later deposited in city dump sites.

It was soon after the night in February, when Amy Lafitte reigned as Queen of the Pirates Ball, that the entire Lafitte family got together and decided to take a two month world cruise.

Serena had sent her flying carriage on ahead to London. There was no way she'd make a return trip on the Splendor at Sea cruise ship no matter how luxurious it was and it was definitely a first class ship. Anyway most tourists wanted to get home as fast as possible when the tour was over.

The minute Amy returned home she couldn't wait to tell Jimmy, her dear friend, all the news about her trip and talk about their new business venture. It was now only the end of April but two months away felt like forever! She turned nineteen years of age right after the ball and now, with all the traveling she'd done, considered herself a world traveler.

The next morning Amy woke up...late. Leaping out of bed she dressed quickly in navy sweats. A quick check in the mirror was about as much as Amy liked looking at herself. She had braided her long silky black hair into a braid over her left shoulder. Dark eyes looked through long lashes that swept a fair complexion with naturally rosy cheeks. She figured her eyes and hair came from the Lafitte side of the family and her fair complexion was thanks to an English Mother.

Last night they spoke briefly about the detective agency but they needed to finalize the details. She told Jimmy to come by for breakfast that now qualified for lunch.

She found him in the small cozy library. There was a huge wood fire blazing. He was sitting in an oversized wing chair. Since he wasn't quite five feet tall his legs stuck out straight in front of him, which she found very endearing. His red hair stuck up in the back, just as she remembered it, and he was wearing his Leprechaun day clothes. And almost everyone, tourist or residents of the Quarter, didn't stop to stare. Because after all just about everyone wore strange clothes in the French Quarter.

"Ah, the world traveler is back!" He had missed her. He struggled out of the wing chair and pretended to be busy stoking the fire to avoid looking at her. She actually looked great!

"Jimmy! We had a really great adventure!"

"Thank you for all the postcards. I felt like I was there, too."

"I wish you had been. I missed you terribly!" She smiled at her friend. "We took a river cruise on the Thames. Everyone we met told Lafitte, he definitely wants everyone to call him Lafitte, anyway they all said that he looked like the real thing. He said he knows that and gets a lot of work playing the pirate, Jean Lafitte."

Jimmy smiled. "That must have been something to see since he is the real Jean Lafitte! And how about your Grandmother? She never leaves her house in the French Quarter and now she's a world traveler."

"Granny was very careful not to make anything appear and disappear in public. Oh, by the way, she wants everyone to call her Serena. She said if Lafitte is to be called Lafitte and not Granddad, since it's all so new to him, then she wants to be called Serena. She said it's just a name and she's very used to Serena. But she added she is still my Granny! Now let me tell you she only did one little magic thing on the entire trip. Lafitte wanted beignets with his afternoon tea so she made them appear. Except for our family everyone else around our table was really amazed and asked where she had found them. Serena said she had bought them in London but when asked where she said she couldn't remember. Old age, she said, which was very funny since she much be about three hundred years old."

"She doesn't look a day over two hundred and for Heaven's sake don't tell her I said that!"

"You know we took Polly Parrot with us! She was over the top being in London again and flew all over squawking and beating her wings in joy. Annie was ever so put out that she had to stay home but Serena said if they took Annie to London she would have to give up her tail. A dog with a monkey tail would attract too much attention. Annie said no way was she doing that. Serena had to promise Annie she could fly like Polly when we got back."

"Does she fly now?" Jimmy grinned trying to imagine the little black and white Terrier mix with wings.

"NO! Even Annie thought she looked just too weird with wings!"

"By the way...where's everyone?"

"Sleeping! We got in this morning. Serena told me there was turbulence over the Atlantic but I slept through the bad part! Thanks goodness! I love flying, just not when the carriage goes up and down and sideways!

"Aw, no rolling meal and drink service?"

"We had meals, Jimmy. Stop being a pain! Serena bought a huge picnic hamper with tons of tasty things from Harrods in London for our trip back home. They have this incredible deli!"

"No more talk about food or I'll be hungry again! On to business. I've been busy since we talked last night."

"Serena told me something I think is important. Do you know anything about her? Like her past?"

"Are you kidding? Not a thing. Serena is a closed book. Until you showed up she never left her house. Now that says it all."

"My Dad said he loved her and was sorry he left her but when she turned the Cajun boys into rats he knew their relatives would come looking for him so he left town and got as far away as possible. He said at first he was really angry because Serena had taken over and didn't let him handle his own problems. Over time he was sorry and wanted to come home, bringing me and Mum with him. They planned to return to New Orleans but then the accident on the cruise ship happened. He said he'd been told all the woman and children on the ship had died. He never gave up hope but there was nothing to go on. It was like hitting a brick wall."

"Wow!"

"Serena had never told anyone her life story before now. She said her Father, Alain Chauvin, had been a very wealthy planter. When he died in a carriage accident his relatives threw her Mother, along with Serena and her younger brother, Marco, out of the plantation and closed ranks around the Chauvin money. Their Father had been a very powerful warlock and he passed down his powers to Marco, who was very young at the time. Serena was given a crystal ball. But she said she knew she could learn to use the crystal ball and have limited powers of her own. Nothing like what Marco inherited, as a Chauvin male, but enough to help her in the world. After all she, too, carried the Chauvin bloodline in her veins."

"Wow!"

"Jimmy could you stop saying 'Wow!'"

"Ok. It's just that if Marco Chauvin is her brother, he's a very powerful warlock in the Quarter."

"Serena said her Mom was very beautiful and immediately secured work in the kitchen of Governor Claiborne. Serena was fifteen and Marco was only five years old. They had to promise to never leave the attic. Her Mom also showed her how to move about the house using the secret doors, next to the fireplaces, that led to passageways going to all the rooms. Serena said as the years passed Marco started showing a dark side that was very disturbing."

"Waa...ah... I had no idea."

"She said her Mom died during a Yellow Fever epidemic. Serena said she applied for kitchen work knowing they would need someone to take her Mom's place. She was hired immediately. That evening, when she returned to the attic, Marco was gone."

"But he was only a young boy."

"He was eight years old. Serena told us how she found out that Marco slept on benches in Jackson Square and ate out of restaurant trash cans. No matter how she tried to find him he was always one step ahead of her. One day he caught the attention of Marie Laveaux. Even young she recognized his aura of power. She took him to her rooms in the Quarter and treated him like her own son and taught him all she knew. Serena said Marie Laveaux was later known in history books as the Queen of the Vampires in New Orleans."

"After Marie Laveaux died Marco acquired a huge following in the Quarter. Marie Laveaux's grave is in the St. Louis Cemetery off Rampart. People still leave notes and flowers for her."

"Serena told me that at the Ghost Ball, when she and my Dad reunited, he told her he was really sorry he hadn't contacted her all those years. Serena said, at that moment, she saw Marco across the room. He pulled off his mask and glared at her. Serena said her brother never thought her son or Lafitte would return. Before she had limited powers but now that her son was alive they would be an even stronger force. I didn't know that even if you're immortal you can die by fire or water. She warned me about Marco. But she said we couldn't live in fear and until he started something she wanted to put the thought aside."

"Let's do just that!" Jimmy didn't want Amy to know how terrified he was of Marco Chauvin. The man was pure evil.

"Jimmy, last night I overheard a family discussion in the library. They thought I was asleep. Serena sounded very serious. She told Mom that as long as she refused to become immortal then she feared for her safety because Marco was out to harm anyone she loved. Mom and Dad had talked this over on the cruise and Dad had told Lafitte that they were not staying in New Orleans. He said he and my mom were leaving for the Caribbean island where Dad had lived for all those years. He still has business interests there. They would come back to visit at Christmas and make surprise visits during the year. They said I would stay with Serena because they knew how close I was to her. Serena said she would not let anything happen to me. And I can visit Mom and Dad anytime I wanted to in the flying carriage."

Jimmy was relieved that Amy was not leaving. He smiled. I have something for you!"

"What?"

He handed her a card saying HAPPY 19TH BIRTHDAY on the front and a hand drawn picture of Jimmy and his brothers on the inside. They had all signed it. "I didn't forget."

Amy held it to her heart. "Oh, thank you! We left so fast after Mardi Gras I forgot about my birthday this year."

"Next year we'll have a really big party."

"When is your birthday, Jimmy? How old are you?"

"Oh, no! After 275 I stopped counting."

He looked so serious Amy started laughing. "Would you like some tea?"

"Yes and some of those little roast beef sandwiches and if there are any around I wouldn't object to a few little tidbits from that Harrods Deli basket you told me about."

Clapping her hands she rushed out of the room. Only Jimmy could take away the darkness and make the sun come out, "I think we ate everything but we shall see!"

She returned from the kitchen with a tray. "Sorry, but there was nothing left in the Harrods basket but Marie put together some of those little roast beef sandwiches you like so much and of course, tea and biscuits."

Jimmy was busy writing copious notes about something that held his interest but not too busy to reach out and grab a little finger sandwich.

She plopped down in a leather overstuffed chair. "So, what's up?"

Closing the notebook with a snap he grinned. "Do you know what we need?"

"An ottoman for my feet!" Amy lifted her feet in the air. "Oh, let me just rush to put that on the list with the thousand other things starting with a problem to solve and paying clients for our new business. Also someone to answer the phones would be nice."

"Don't forget an office with our names on the door." Amy smiled. No one made her laugh like her good friend.

"I think I solved that one. This morning on my way over here I saw Suzie putting a For Rent sign in the window of The Sweet Shop."

"What a great location!" Amy sat forward in her chair.

"I thought so, too, so I went in and asked her if she would hold it until I talked to you. I did say I was sure you'd be thrilled. And I also mentioned we were starting The French Quarter Detective Agency. Just a working title for now."

"Wonderful! I believe in getting the word out right away. And it has that store room with the brick wall."

"We'll have lots of clients from Pirates Village, too."

"Jimmy, let's call her."

"Do you still have her phone number?"

"I do…somewhere." Amy rushed out of the room. She returned shortly waving a piece of paper.

Jimmy dialed the number. "Suzie, hi, we're definitely taking the shop. We'll be there shortly to sign the lease."

He said yes a few times and then hung up.

"We have good news, too!"

"What did she say?"

"Two sisters, Lynne and Gayle, they live in the Garden District, anyway they stopped by on their way back from Café du Monde and noticed the sign was out of the window. Suzie told them the shop was going to be leased to The French Quarter Detective Agency and what a surprise because they said that just that morning they had been talking about finding someone to locate a relative who is missing along with a family heirloom…a treasure map! Amy, me dear, we might have our first client!"

"Let's go see Suzie!"

They arrived just as Suzie was putting the last packing box in a van.

Suzie explained that the lease included all utilities, phone, cable and the apartment with bath upstairs, that was now used to hold boxes.

Amy was excited, rushing around looking at everything. She told Jimmy that the apartment upstairs had great potential.

When she returned to the main room downstairs Jimmy was folding the signed lease and tucking it away. Suzie wished them well and left.

"Let's write an ad for the receptionist." Amy sat on a box full of sweets that Suzie said they could have since there was no more room in the van.

"I'm ahead of you on that. What about this." Jimmy read from his notebook.

RECEPTIONIST NEEDED for The French Quarter Detective Agency.

**Apply in person tomorrow at 10 AM at The
Sweet Shop, corner of Pirates Alley across from
Jackson Square.**

"I like it."

Jimmy called and read the ad into the phone that Suzie had thoughtfully put in their business name, The French Quarter Detective Agency. He was assured it would run for a week in the French Quarter Gazette starting tomorrow. They were in luck since the paper was going to print in ten minutes. This hardly gave them enough time to organize their new offices but Jimmy figured they would manage.

"Amy, I've been dying to ask you something, just to make sure it wasn't all my imagination. The night of the Ghost Ball your Dad showed up with his Dad who happens to be the real Jean Lafitte, and then Lafitte gave Serena a diamond ring, that shot fireworks into the sky, to make the whole thing permanent."

"That says it all. When we got back that night my Dad and Lafitte, do not call him Grandfather, he likes to be called Lafitte. Anyway they stayed up for hours explaining everything to Serena and Mom."

"Oh, that must have been something to hear."

"And then we left for the Grand Tour. That sums it up!"

"Since the ad goes in tomorrow morning we need to get organized now."

Amy and Jimmy rushed around putting mostly empty boxes outside for trash pickup.

They talked as they worked.

"I can't believe Suzie left the shop." Amy wiped her forehead with a paper towel.

Jimmy took a little break, sitting on a plastic crate they were using as a temporary chair.

"She told me that after the Murder Mystery Dinner Party the Bed & Breakfast became so successful that Mary asked her to move there and help out. Did you know Suzie is a first cousin to Mary and Delia?"

"I think I heard that. Well that's wonderful for them and for us. You know we have a Murder Mystery Dinner Party rain check anytime we want."

"I know. We'll have to go sometime. They are booked through the summer. And remember Billy Butler?"

"He was with Kathy, right?" Amy remembered the kind nursing student.

"Well Billy plays for the Saints. He went back and told all his friends and they totally took the entire B&B for the two weeks of

Jazz Fest that's coming up. So Mary added four more en suite bedrooms in the attic."

They gathered any leftover candy they found into boxes they labeled "Free Sweets" and put them all outside the door. The empty boxes they had put out earlier were gone. "Someone must be moving." Amy observed. "And I think we should hang a big sign over the front door declaring we're open for business and our names on the door."

"Amy, I do believe you have a mind for marketing. Let me guess...."

"Yep...from a book. The orphanage had great books on business and marketing."

"Why did I even ask!" Jimmy grumbled.

Amy finished the black lettering on the glass window in the front door.

THE FRENCH QUARTER DETECTIVE AGENCY

Investigators Amy Lafitte and Jimmy O'Brien.

Phone 555-2242

"How do you like it?"

"I'd like it more if my name was first."

"L comes before O." Amy smiled. "We have to go to City Hall and get all the permits we need to operate."

"I'll do that. You just keep organizing things." He hated organizing things and moving boxes around.

"Do you have enough money for the permits?"

"Nah, I'll just find out how much it is and drop some gold dust over---"

"---Jimmy! Don't you dare!"

He laughed. "Oh, all right! You take the fun out of things! "But not to worry...I have real money!" He fast walked out the door and down the street before she found something for him to do. He spent the rest of the afternoon going from one line to another. No wonder Amy was so quick to let him go. The really hard part of starting a business was waiting in the endless lines, for all the permits, to operate legally.

Serena, with Annie right behind her, came through the storeroom into the shop. "I like it!" She stood in the doorway with a hand on her hip.

Amy smiled. "The Lafitte hot line, right?"

"You called your Mother and she called me."

"It doesn't look much like an office right now but I'm working on it."

"Have you thought about what you're going to charge for your detective services?"

"I did. I have more than enough money. At first it was an excuse so I could hang out with Jimmy, who has been a great friend to me, and now I'd just like to help people who needs my help. Serena, I want my life to mean something. To give back. I've been very lucky to have all of my family together again."

Serena smiled. "I'm proud of you."

Amy hugged her.

Before her eyes teared up, something that almost never happened, Serena added, "So, let's get busy. Maybe I can help a bit."

"That would be wonderful." Amy clapped her hands together. "Oh, there's one thing?"

"Yes."

"We need detective credentials to operate."

"Done." With a wave, two framed credentials now hung on the wall.

"Now how do you see it?"

"Well, I would like two desks in the middle, with book cases against both walls, comfortable seating for clients when they walk in, a coffee machine on a table in the back, and a refrigerator for snacks and things."

"Easy to do."

Amy watched in amazement as Serena, with a twist of her wrist and a snap of her fingers, locked the front door, unfurled sheets to cover the windows and the view from anyone passing by, and then furnished the room exactly as Amy had described it with the addition of a colorful rug covering most of the floor.

"Wow, thanks, Serena, it's perfect."

Annie curled up in a doggie bed against the back wall that her Mistress had thoughtfully provided for her when she visited.

"There's a room and bath on the second floor. Would you like me to do something with it? Maybe turn it into a livable space?"

"Oh, thank you so much! That would be great!" Amy had imagined the one bedroom en suite with blue and white gingham cushions and white wicker furniture. Maybe they would hire a receptionist who needed a place to live.

"Let's go look at it."

Returning at mid-afternoon Jimmy found Amy sitting in a desk chair outside the door handing out business cards to everyone that went by. He looked inside. Incredible, he thought. The office looked like a place of business. A bookcase, filled with books, took up one wall. Comfortable sofas and overstuffed chairs were scattered about. There was a coffee machine on a buffet table in the back near the storeroom. There were two desks; one was placed near the front door and one near the back. And two detective certificates allowing them to operate legally.

"Wow! Did my brothers drop by?"

"No, but Serena did. She came through the storeroom and never left the office. She locked the front door and hung sheets in the windows so no one passing by could see the transformation going on inside."

"Good idea."

"Everything is just like I wanted it."

"I can believe that!" Jimmy was running around touching things like he was making sure it wasn't just an illusion of furniture but the real thing.

"Wait until you see the upstairs. Maybe we'll hire someone who needs a place to live."

Jimmy raced upstairs to the former empty space that was now a furnished and newly painted apartment with a new bath. There was also a small closet kitchen.

"Wow!" Jimmy stood there amazed.

Amy was right behind him." Do you like the wicker furniture and the blue cushions?"

"Girl stuff but it all looks fresh."

"There's even a doggy bed."

"There's one downstairs, too."

"Annie was with Serena today and she ran to the little bed the minute she came in. And when you went through the store room did you notice the bicycle she left for us to get around?"

"What is the 'us,' AMY?" Jimmy grumbled.

"It has a little seat for you, too."

Jimmy scrunched up his face. "I have a feeling this is not going to be pretty."

Marching into the store room he yelled....."Oh NO!! I knew it! I knew it! It has a BABY SEAT on the back!"

"That's not a baby seat it's just a seat with a seatbelt so you can ride safely."

Jimmy just looked at Amy and shook his head.

"She also made me promise we would both wear riding helmets. They are in the basket in the front of the bike."

"Oh, sure, why not, I'll look like an idiot in that baby seat. At least with the helmet on no one can see my face. I'm spared that humiliation."

"Let's go for a ride!" Amy shouted out.

"I know I look really silly and don't tell me I don't!" Jimmy climbed into the little seat and strapped the helmet on his head. Amy opened the door to Pirates Alley and away they went.

Mildred had been thinking a lot about that flying carriage she had seen in City Park. That was the day that everything in her world changed. "Another trip?" She watched her husband pack. Gerald was an Engineer and took jobs out of the country all the time.

"Yeah. I'm going to Saudi Arabia."

"That sounds exciting."

"Mildred, let me get to the point. Our whole marriage has never worked out. I didn't tell you but I saw a divorce lawyer last week. I can't believe this trip came at a perfect time."

"Gerald, this is so sudden!" Mildred was stunned. She had always been the perfect wife.

"You'll get the papers in the mail." "I see."

"I'll have someone come by and pick up the rest of my things. The rent is paid until the end of the month. That gives you time to make your own arrangements."

"I see."

"Is that all you can say...I see?"

"What about Bruno?"

The dog was laying on the floor listening to them. Personally he didn't like Gerald. He was cruel, yanked his leash when they walked, and many times forgot to feed him.

"You got him from the SPCA. Bring him back."

Bruno's eyes widened, as did Mildred's.

"I see." Mildred was finally free of Gerald's cruelty but she secretly worried what would happen to them. She and Bruno would shortly be out of a place to live, with no money. She grabbed Bruno's leash and headed out the door. She would think of something. And the best place to think was over coffee at Andy's.

A van pulled up in front of Andy's News Stand on Esplanade just as Mildred got there. A young boy leaped out, grabbed a stack of French Quarter Gazette newspapers and threw the tied bundle on the ground near the door.

Andy came out of the store, cut the twine binding the newspapers and moved a stack under a sign advertising the price and carried the rest inside the store.

Stopping to pick up the latest Gazette she went inside to pay for it. She came out and sat on a concrete bench in front of the store with a cup of café au lait and read the newspaper, just as she had done many times before. Only this time she turned to the Help Wanted section. The French Quarter Detective Agency, Jimmy's ad for a

Receptionist, was the first one she saw. All applicants were to apply in person starting at ten the next morning.

A smile lit up her face. She wasn't too late. "Bruno, this is our lucky day. A Detective Agency is looking for a Receptionist. I can do that. Tomorrow morning we'll go to see about the job."

When they got back to the apartment Gerald was gone. Not even a goodbye note.

The next morning at nine Mildred and Bruno set out for The Sweet Shop. Bruno decided to be on his best behavior. He would sit up and beg. That was a real crowd pleaser, he thought. He prayed that his mistress would get the job and be able to take him to work with her every day.

It was a long walk. Mildred decided that one of her first purchases would be a bicycle, with a basket, for Bruno to ride in but first she needed a place to live. She bent down and patted Bruno's head. She was surprised that she was acting like she had the job but she had to stay positive.

Amy and Jimmy arrived at their new office with only minutes to spare before there was a knock on the glass door.

Candy Malone was the first to apply for the job. She snapped her gum and wore high heels. Not the sort Amy had been hoping would apply.

The interview ended quickly when Jimmy suggested she put her hand on the brick wall in the storeroom and nothing happened. Being able to go back and forth to Pirate Village was a number one requirement.

Becky Street was next. The minute she started telling Amy she had to take fifteen minute breaks every two hours, a one hour lunch out of the office and she couldn't work past three in the afternoon that interview ended.

Mildred wondered how long the ad had been running in the paper. She was relieved to see that the *"Receptionist Wanted"* sign in was still in the front window. They hadn't hired anyone...yet. She gently opened the door and walked in.

Amy and Jimmy looked at each other the minute Mildred entered. They immediately liked her easy going nature.

Mildred just stood there. She wanted to say something perfect...something that would get her the job.

"You're here for the job?"

"Yes. My name is Mildred." Not a brilliant reply but the only one she could think of.

"Come on in. I'm Amy." Amy stepped back so Mildred could pass with her dog in tow. "What a sweet little guy!" Amy bent down to pat the little black and white English Bulldog's head.

Bruno went into a flurry of movement. Sitting on his back legs he pawed the air begging silently. *Miss Amy, please hire my Mistress. We have no money and nowhere to live. My Mistress is wonderful to me. She never yells or anything. My name is Bruno and I can do tricks.*

I hear you, Bruno. Amy soundlessly answered back.

Amy smiled and stood up. Bruno was so excited he started spinning around. *Miss Amy, you can hear me! Thank you! Thank you!*

Mildred wondered what had gotten into her usually sweet and very docile little dog.

"My name is Mildred. I've never been a Receptionist but I know I can do the job."

"You're hired." Amy knew instinctively that Mildred would be perfect for the job.

"What?" Jimmy yelled from in back of the store.

"I just said I hired...Mildred." She yelled back.

Jimmy quickly joined them. "Amy, I'd just like to ask a question!" Jimmy looked totally bewildered but at the same time, totally thrilled that maybe they didn't have to do any more hiring or talking about the job to any more applicants.

"Okay."

"Mildred, right? Mildred, do you have any pirates in your family tree?" Jimmy asked.

"I don't know."

"That's really important, AMY!" He shouted her name in frustration.

"Yes, I guess it is."

"Mildred, would you come this way." Jimmy led the way to the storeroom. He opened the door and led the way over to the hand print on the brick wall. "Mildred, do you see that hand print on the wall? Would you put your hand, palm side down, in the hand on the wall."

"Sure." Mildred did so and a door appeared. "Where did that come from?" She jumped back.

When no one passed through, the door disappeared, and the wall went back the way it was.

"Well that's a relief!" Amy looked at Jimmy and smiled. She led the way back to her desk, talking as she walked. "I just have a few other things about the job to talk about. Take a seat."

"Thank you." Mildred sat down across from Amy.

"Did you ask about her salary requirements? Jimmy yelled from the store room.

Amy rolled her eyes. "I was just going to ask."

"So?" Jimmy yelled again.

"Jimmy stop yelling!" She turned to their new Receptionist. "Mildred---"

"---actually, I like the name Milly better. Milly Foster." That just sort of popped into her head. For as long as she could remember she wanted to be called Milly. And Foster had been her maiden name. Now was her chance. New life, new name!

"Okay, Milly Foster it is." Amy winked at Bruno who was sitting on his back legs, fanning the air with his little front paws, and praying. "By the way we have a totally furnished apartment with bath on the second floor that goes with the job, if you're interested. Oh, and that includes all utilities, internet, cable and phone, and it includes linens, towels and everything you might need in the kitchen, too."

"That's like a dream come true! But I don't know if I can afford it. How much would that be?"

"I'll tell you what...no charge until you get your life organized. And there's no time limit. So back to the question of salary. What did you have in mind?"

For once in her life she felt secure and happy. She would have worked for free but she couldn't say that. "What about one hundred dollars a week? Is that too much?"

Jimmy fast walked into the office from the store room when he heard this. "Even I'm not that cheap. How about two hundred a week?"

"Oh, yes, thank you!"

"And you get a free business cell phone in case you need to reach us."

"Yes! Everything is perfect." Milly lowered her head and bent over, using the excuse of scratching Bruno's ears, she added in a soft voice, "I am very grateful for the apartment, too."

"Hours are nine to five. Can you start work tomorrow?" "Oh yes, we can....uh, I mean me and Bruno. Is it okay...my having Bruno?" Milly held her breath. She loved the little dog and would have turned down the job if she couldn't have him with her.

"Of course. I love dogs and Bruno." *Bruno, you are especially sweet.*

Oh, thank you, Miss Amy! Bruno was spinning around with joy.

Milly wondered again what had gotten into Bruno. He was usually so quiet. What was weird was that he was acting like he understood everything Amy was saying. Now that's just downright crazy, Milly thought.

"Move in anytime you want and we'll see you tomorrow." Amy handed Milly three keys. "One for the front door, back door and one for the apartment. You can get to the apartment from the stairs in the store room. Why don't you go check it out?"

She put the two keys in her backpack. "Thank you so much. I don't need to see it. I know the apartment will be lovely. I don't have many things so I'm very grateful that it's furnished, too. I'll be back first thing in morning." Milly and Bruno left in haste.

Amy took the Receptionist Wanted sign out of the window and turned to Jimmy. "Are we lucky or what?"

The office phone rang. Amy answered, spoke briefly and had a big smile when she hung up. "This is an incredible day. Lynne and Gayle Robichaux, the sisters who inquired about the detective agency just called. They will be here tomorrow morning at ten. From what they said their nephew disappeared, along with their treasure map."

"I love a good mystery." Milly looked down, finally unclenching her fingers.

"So do I." Amy smiled.

CHAPTER TWO

First Case for The French Quarter Detective Agency

Bruno was relieved when Milly picked him up and carried him. His short English Bulldog legs would never have kept up with his mistress' fast walk back to their old apartment.

It was eerily quiet inside. Bruno rejoiced that Gerald was gone for good. They were going to a far better life with really nice people.

While his mistress packed Bruno rushed around assembling his few things into a pile by the front door. He checked off his list: fuzzy rubber caterpillar that squeaked, a round rubber blow fish that had lost its squeaker, two rawhide bones, almost as big as he was, a box of bacon treats, a bright red rubber ball and a tug-of-war rope. Not a lot for a lifetime but what he had he loved. And most of all he loved Milly. He had been a little orphan who had lucked out when Milly found him at the SPCA.

Milly had a duffel bag on wheels. First she packed Bruno's things which included his stainless steel water and dog food bowls, one bag of dry dog food and his toys. She then packed her few things. She had noticed a doggie bed at the back of the office so she left Bruno's hard cushion behind. Smiling she dropped it back in the corner. Let Gerald's packers worry about what to do with the old thing.

She left a note on the kitchen table wishing Gerald a happy life. She had stopped at the post office on the way home and filled out a change of address form.

Reaching around the back of the refrigerator she removed an envelope that had been taped out of sight, with a small nest egg of cash. Tomorrow morning she'd call a cab and arrive in at her new life in comfort. For the first time she actually slept peacefully.

It was dark before Amy finally locked the back door leading to Pirate's Alley and climbed on the new bike. Jimmy, not easily, finally climbed into his seat on the back. He reluctantly grumbled, "This beats walking!"

"Jimmy, want to come for dinner? We can tell everybody about our great first day."

"I wish I could but Aunt Maggie is leaving tonight and I promised to be there. All my brothers are home for the take off. She loves hopping on her carpet and flying off. It's really something to see!"

"Tell Aunt Maggie bye for me. I'll see her next time."

"Okay."

Amy dropped Jimmy off in front of the Golden Palace Hotel. She knew he was headed for the tropical garden and the secret door that led down an underground tunnel to Leprechaun City and home.

It wasn't far to the Lodge. To her surprise only Marie was waiting up for her.

"Where's everyone?"

"Well your Mom and Dad went to hear a new Jazz group at Preservation Hall. Serena and Lafitte said they were going out to dinner and then to their house. So it's just you and me."

"I'm not hungry, Marie. I think I'll just go to bed."

"I'll bring a little something to your room."

"Okay."

Amy had spent the last two months with her family. She didn't mind the quiet.

She showered and started to climb into bed when she saw the tray with little finger sandwiches, a stack of cookies and a large glass of milk that Marie had left for her. Good thing she didn't say she was really hungry, Amy smiled.

Amy dressed and left early the next morning. She loved riding her new bike. Stopping for beignets at Cafe du Monde she headed for their office right across Jackson Square.

The smell of chicory coffee was in the air, the fax machine was humming, the phone was ringing, and Milly was handling everything like she had been doing it forever. Bruno was very happy lying in his new doggie bed in the back.

Amy stuck her head in the front door. "How do you like the apartment?"

"I love it!" Milly had a mile wide smile. Bruno twirled around in his doggie bed. Milly gave him an odd look. It was crazy to think he understood what Amy had just said. "Bruno does, too."

"I know. I'll be right back."

Their first clients were talking to Milly when Amy returned from the storeroom where she stored her bike.

"We're early!" They both said at once.
"No problem."

"Your charming receptionist makes coffee with chicory better than Cafe Du Monde."

Amy smiled gratefully at Milly who was busy at the front desk but managed to keep her eyes down and smile at the same time. "Please have a seat." Amy sat behind her desk and indicated the two chairs for clients. Just as she was wondering where Jimmy was he came in the front door, said hello to everyone, and headed towards the coffee machine.

"That's Jimmy O'Brien, my partner in crime." Amy smiled. The ladies quickly sat down.

"I'm Lynne Robichaux and that's Gayle. Our nephew has been missing for a year---"

"---Lynne, it's been not quite a year." Gayle quietly added.

"Yes, well, it could be two months and we'd be worried. Bugs, that's our nephew, Bugs Robichaux, he inherited an island, Castle Island, somewhere off Key West, Florida, not quite a year ago. We inherited a pirate treasure map and the treasure is somewhere on the island." Lynne started searching her large handbag. "I have it somewhere."

"Don't forget about the Castle on the island." Gayle spoke up. "We had no idea! Apparently it's a huge castle and it has been rented to a Reverend and his wife and the will states that if the island is sold they have first offer. Very complicated. Anyway, we had to work together, you see." Gayle touched Lynne's arm whose attention was still on searching her purse. "It's our treasure but the Castle and island belong to Bugs and since getting to the island is by boat and we get seasick, Bugs said he would go, find the treasure for us, and decide what he wanted to do with his property at the same time. But then he didn't come back."

Lynne placed a large manila envelope on the desk. "Look, Gayle, I found it! We collected everything you might need." She pulled a hand drawn map from the envelope. "This is for you. I made copies before Bugs left."

"Great." Amy reached for the map.

"There's more." Lynne handed her one hand written page after another. "Here's a list of his cell phone calls before he left. After he arrived in Key West his cell phone wasn't used again. I included his credit card expenses, which also stopped. I included a list of his friends if that would help. Although we did call them, nothing came from it. They didn't even know he had left New Orleans." Lynne reached into her large bag and pulled out a lap computer. "We thought maybe his emails might help, but nothing. We received a postcard from Key West when he first arrived but then nothing until he sent a postcard saying he sold Castle Island but he didn't mention the treasure. That is not like him at all. Here's a picture of Bugs. It was taken right before he left."

Amy reached for the picture. Bugs was a handsome young man. He had light brown hair and wore glasses. He looked like a young college professor. He was slim and about six feet tall. In the picture he was standing next to his VW Beetle. "Early twenties?" Amy asked.

Lynne, who seemed to be the spokesperson, continued. "Twenty-one. He has one semester left before he graduates from Loyola."

"Did you contact the Key West Police?

"We did!" They said in unison.

"Two months after the postcard saying he had sold the island we called and talked to Chief Barker. He took a missing person report and said he'd have it checked out right away. He called us back. He said he had personally gone out to Castle Island. A Reverend and his wife are living there. They said they bought the property for two million dollars in cash, almost a year ago from Bugs who seemed thrilled with the sale and said he was going to buy a sailboat and go around the world which is very strange because Bugs doesn't like sailing. He says it's too slow." Gayle nodded in agreement. "Anyway we asked about the sale and Chief Barker sent us a copy of the Bill of Sale. He told us it had been witnessed by two prominent Key West residents. Chief Barker paid them a visit. Apparently it was all done legally." Lynne pulled legal papers out of her bag and handed them to Amy.

"Interesting." Amy didn't see anything amiss in the paperwork.

Jimmy joined them. He picked up Bugs' picture and studied it.

"We will find Bugs." Amy assured the ladies. "If I need anything else I have your address and phone."

"One last thing." Lynne pulled a large envelope from her purse and placed it in front of Amy. "There's Ten Thousand Dollars in cash and a credit card for expenses. Would that be enough for now?"

"It's much more than we would charge." Amy realized she hadn't talked to Jimmy about not charging for their services.

"We can afford it. All we want is to have Bugs back home safely. Our only brother and his wife died when Bugs was quite young." Gayle added, "Yes, quite young, and he came to live with us in the family home. He's like a son to us."

Jimmy knew the ladies would never take the money back. They needed hope. Paying right now meant there was hope. He reached over and picked up the envelope. "This goes into our vault. I'll take care of it right now." Jimmy went to the back of the office into the storeroom, shutting the door behind him.

"I promise I will find Bugs." Amy smiled kindly at Lynne.

I know you will, dear, I know you will." Lynne patted Amy's hand. Suzie recommended you. Did she tell you we went to school with her?"

"Now would that be...Dominican." Amy smiled

"Oh, yes! How did you know?"

"Lucky guess!" Just about every woman she'd met starting at the Devereux Plantation Murder Mystery Dinner Party had gone to Dominican.

"Your partner in crime is so colorfully dressed!" Lynne looked towards the back of the office.

"He's a Leprechaun. A tall Leprechaun." Amy wasn't sure what to say.

Milly, who had been sitting quietly until now, quickly added. "It's the Quarter, you know. This morning on the way over here I saw two young men dressed like vampires, black cloaks and all!"

Gayle clapped her hands. "Don't you just love it. They are all over the Quarter. They run the Vampire Tours. Have you been to the Royal Palace Hotel? They said on Mardi Gras night there was a glass elevator on the roof taking guests way up in the sky to a secret party. The rumor is that all the guests attending were pirate ghosts! They've added that hotel to the Haunted Hotels Tour in the Quarter."

Amy's eyes widened. She called out to Jimmy who was fast walking to the storeroom to keep from laughing out loud. "Isn't that wild, Jimmy, pirate ghosts!"

Lynne hadn't given up on talking about Jimmy. "He's not what you think of a Leprechaun, but he does dress like one. I always thought Leprechauns were very tiny...little people."

Like he could hear through walls Jimmy came back from the storeroom smiling. "Not my family. We're all tall. I'm almost four feet tall and I'm not even the tallest. I have two brothers who are taller. It's a clan thing!"

"Oh, I see." Lynne looked mortified. She hoped he hadn't been insulted. She liked them both and felt if anyone could find Bugs they could. "Well, I like you both and I know you will find our nephew."

The sisters collected their things and left the office. Amy turned to find Jimmy busy reading over all the information they had on Bugs. She didn't care how tall he was he was her best friend. "We are going to Key West, Florida. "Milly could you make arrangements for us on the first flight out in the morning."

"Sure. I'll get on it right away. Monday is a huge travel day out of New Orleans."

"I know all this has been rushed but will you be okay with us gone."

"Don't worry about anything here."

"I'm sure Serena, that's my Granny, will come and visit. She has a little dog named Annie. Bruno might make a friend."

Bruno raised his head at the sound of his name. Annie? A little female dog? He knew by the smell on the doggie bed that she had been here at least once. And now he had a name...Annie! How wonderful to make a new friend!

Don't worry, Bruno. I'll ask Serena to bring Annie with her to visit. Amy sent a silent message to the little dog who was wagging his tail with enthusiasm.

Amy and Jimmy were busy for the rest of the day. They had a lot to show Milly about Pirates Village. He showed her how to come and go through the magical wall. Getting organized in one day was a challenge. By the end of the day Amy was sure Milly was well prepared to handle anything and Jimmy noted that nothing fazed her so they were both sure she was the perfect receptionist.

Amy suggested they knock off for the day since Milly had booked a noon flight for them the next day nonstop to Miami where they'd change planes for a commuter to Key West.

"Our first case!" Jimmy didn't even grumble as he climbed into his little seat on the back of the bike. "Amy, you know you could go to Florida and take care of this and I could stay here and run the office."

"Milly does that quite well."

"Well, I could stay here and handle new business that comes in."

"Milly will call us on the phone if something comes up." "Uh, Uh..."

"Jimmy, are you saying you want me to go alone? "Well, yes."

"Why?"

"With Maggie gone my brothers are a bit wild."

"How about this? You come on the first case and then I'll handle things on my own from then on. Just so I get the hang of things. AND I know that is the first thing Serena is going to ask you. She will make sure you are going with me."

"Okay, deal."

Earlier she had talked Jimmy into coming to dinner. She wasn't sure what her Mom and Dad would say about her going off to Florida when she was just getting settled into her new life but she knew with Jimmy there he would handle all the questions she was sure the family had. And now she had alerted him about Serena which he probably knew anyway.

She left Jimmy in the kitchen trying to get Melita to make him some before dinner snacks. Hearing voices in the sitting room she walked in. Serena and Lafitte were busy at a table in the adjacent study filled with little buildings and something that looked like miniature carnival rides.

"Hi. What is that?"

"It's a plan for a new Ponchatrain Beach!"

"What happened to the old one?"

"It went out of business years ago."

Lafitte laughed. "Serena decided that we need a new one."

"What will it look like?"

"It will have the same rides: The Big Zephyr Rollercoaster, game booths, sky rides, a huge Carousel, great restaurants and an amphitheater on the beach for nighttime shows. We're designing the Haunted House of Mirrors right now. Our Ponchatrain Beach will be a cross between a small town Carny and Disneyland.

"Wow! It sounds great!"

"As you enter the park you have to go through turnstiles with hand passes something like Pirates Village. The location will be on the site of the old Ponchatrain Beach which is now just acres and acres of weeds on Lake Ponchatrain. And you can swim in our unpolluted Lake Ponchatrain, too."

"Oh, Serena, it sounds wonderful! I have some exciting news, too. We have our first mystery to solve. We're leaving tomorrow morning for Miami."

Serena gave her a very serious look. "Jimmy is going with you, right?"

"Oh definitely!"

"My darling granddaughter, remember if you need me..."

"I know, Serena. Thank you. Oh, by the way, we hired a fantastic receptionist to run the office while we're gone. Her name is Milly. She has a really sweet dog named Bruno. Do you think you might drop by and bring Annie...Bruno asked."

"Of course. And I would like to see Milly again. I saw her once in City Park. I'm so glad you have her in charge of your office."

Amy wanted to know more about how she knew Milly but she could see they were busy with their new Ponchatrain Beach project. "I'll leave you to your design. I can't wait to see it when I come back."

Serena smiled. "It will be some time before we get this all sorted out. Lafitte keeps changing his mind. One thing we will have is a cafe that has the best hot roast beef Po'boys and of course, oyster and shrimp Po'boys.

Amy laughed. "I love it!"

The minute Amy left the room Serena pulled a bell that rang in the kitchen. Marie quickly answered the call.

She spoke privately to Marie. "I want you to tell Jimmy that under no circumstances should any harm come to Amy. She is strong willed and very competent but she is still finding her way in the world."

Marie nodded her head and brought her message to Jimmy. He nodded in agreement. No one crossed Serena.

Amy's Mom and Dad came home at seven, in time for dinner. They had a million questions to ask about the new detective agency and the first clients. Amy was glad Jimmy was there. After dinner she walked Jimmy to the door, trying to suppress a huge yawn.

"See you tomorrow." Jimmy shrugged into his jacket for the walk home.

"I'll pick you up in front of the hotel at eight. Be ready, Jimmy. It takes forever to get to the airport and there's security."

Jimmy smiled. Like Amy knew so much about flying and airport security. One trip and she was a world traveler. "Yes, Ma'am!"

The next morning Amy was at the hotel at eight sharp. Jimmy was waiting in front with a backpack over his shoulder and two plane tickets in his right hand. He was also wearing jeans, a t-shirt and a navy blazer. Amy was amazed.

"Hey, where are your usual clothes?"

Jimmy got into the yellow cab next to Amy in the backseat. "Are you serious? In the Quarter no one pays attention but outside of our world here, everyone stares. I want to blend in."

"I see." Amy looked at Jimmy with his bright red hair sticking up in the back as usual. Oh yeah, he'd blend in!

CHAPTER THREE

Amy Meets Harry

The agent at the gate handed Amy their boarding passes. "You have the last two seats. I'm sorry they can't be together but you have one by the window and one on the aisle in the row behind you. You better hurry. You're the last ones. They're shutting the doors anytime now."

Jimmy grumbled. "I want the aisle. I always fly aisle. And we're not together. I am not happy."

Amy turned and spoke calmly to Jimmy whose face was as bright red as his hair. "You have an aisle seat only you're right behind me. We have to change planes in Miami so maybe we'll be next to each other on that flight." Amy did her best to reassure him as they quickly headed down the hallway to the plane that was boarding.

"I bet the plane from Miami to Key West is so small we'll probably be in rows of single seats."

"Well there you go that's an aisle seat!" Amy quickly changed the subject. "Maybe the person next to me will change seats with you once we take off."

"And maybe they won't." He huffed.

63

"Jimmy...don't do anything!"

He continued complaining all the way to their seats.

The aisle seat next to Amy was already taken by a man with a baseball cap tipped over his forehead. She carefully climbed over his outstretched legs. He appeared to be sleeping but she could see he was watching her. The flight attendants started to advise everyone about plane procedure and preparing for takeoff.

Jimmy had no choice but to take the aisle seat in the row behind Amy.

He whispered through the crack between the seats in front of him. "I'm going to meditate right now. Can't move until the seat belt sign is off, anyway."

Amy smiled. He told her on the way to the airport that he hated flying. She hoped the meditating would help. She looked out the small window by her side and wondered how his current seatmate would deal with the low hum Jimmy made when he meditated.

Her seatmate raised his baseball cap and looked her over. "I'm Harry Morgan." He shoved his baseball cap in a pack under his seat.

Amy turned to look at him. She liked the way a lock of dark brown hair, with mahogany streaks, fell over his forehead. And his eyes...dark blue like the Irish Sea. Amy's heart skipped a beat. He was really cute! He was wearing khaki pants, a white t-shirt and a well-worn dark brown leather flying jacket. He looked like a young Marlon Brando. "*Streetcar Named Desire*" had been one of her favorite movies at the orphanage.

She smiled. "Amy Lafitte. My friend behind you is Jimmy O'Brien. He's hoping you will change seats with him after we take off." Which they were doing right now.

"Sure, but if I do that I'll miss getting to know you." Amy really liked his easy going manner.

Amy whispered, "You never know he might fall asleep and forget about changing seats." Whenever Jimmy mediated he usually fell sound asleep so anything was possible. "Where are you from, Harry?"

"Originally from Massachusetts. Right now I work for my Dad at Morgan Air in Miami. I just delivered a float plane to a buyer in Louisiana."

"A pilot. That's wonderful. I feel safe already."
"No problem. This is an easy flight."

At that moment the plane bounced a little. Amy hoped Jimmy was fast asleep.

"Just a little turbulence. You can expect that flying out of New Orleans. We'll be at cruising altitude in no time."

"Fantastic." Amy again peered back between the seats. "My friend is definitely asleep."

"Tell me about yourself." Harry smiled. He wanted to get to know Amy Lafitte.

Amy smiled. "Jimmy and I just started a detective agency in the French Quarter. We're on our first case. Our first clients asked us to find their nephew who left a year ago for Key West, with their Pirate Treasure Map, and never came back. "

"A lady detective! Wow! Do you have any clues to go on?" "We have a copy of the map. The treasure is somewhere on Castle Island, a private island off Key West. Our clients inherited the map and their nephew inherited the private island. They got a postcard when he got to Key West. He said he had rented a boat and was heading to the island. Later they got the last postcard saying he had sold Castle Island then he just disappeared. Maybe someone remembers renting a boat to Bugs. That's his name, Bugs Robichaux. The map shows the island is somewhere between Key West and the Bahamas."

"In the Bermuda Triangle?"

Amy nodded her head. "I try not to think about that. Our clients put in a missing persons report to the Key West Police. They looked into it but said he sold the island, took the cash and disappeared."

"Are you from New Orleans?"

"My family is there. I was born in London and spent thirteen years on an island off Scotland."

"A world traveler!" *You are definitely interesting, Ms. Lafitte. And funny and smart and gorgeous. Wow!*

Amy heard his silent thoughts. She wondered what Harry would say if he knew the whole story about her "interesting" family.

"Are you going to rent a boat in Key West?"

"Those are the plans."

"Maybe I can help. I know everyone in boat rentals."

"Thanks, Harry. I've never been to Florida before."

"I also know the Police Chief in Key West. I'm going there myself. I keep my fishing boat at the Key West Marina. I have to do some minor repairs on it. I was going to stop by my house and pick up my car in Miami then drive to Key West. You and Jimmy are welcome to drive with me and if you don't mind waiting for a few hours I can get my boat ready and I can take you to find the island you're looking for."

Amy had a really good feeling about Harry. "That would be fantastic! Do you have the time for all that?"

"Sure. I don't have to fly for a few weeks."

"Then I definitely accept and thank you. To tell you the truth I was dreading that puddle jumper to Key West."

Harry laughed. "Everyone calls it Fright Airways. That's why I drive there instead of flying."

Just then they both heard Jimmy snoring in the aisle seat behind them.

Amy looked out the window to cover a smile. Now they had time to get to know each other. "How long have you been transporting planes?"

"I started learning to fly when I was young. By the time I got to High School I was qualified to fly anything. I graduated from the University of Massachusetts last May and went to work for my Dad. I love flying planes to buyers where I can have a stopover in New Orleans on my way home."

"It really is a magical place." Amy wondered if he knew just how magical it really was.

"I'll have more reason to stop there now."

Amy held her breath and asked, "Do you have any pirates in your family tree?"

Harry smiled. "I do! But now that I think of it...Amy Lafitte...are you related to Jean Lafitte?"

"He's my Grandfather." The minute she said it she wanted to take it back.

"Very funny. You must get that question all the time."

"I do."

"Well somewhere in my family tree is the pirate Edward Teach...Blackbeard."

"He was from North Carolina."

"I know. I'm amazed to meet someone who knows about pirates. I think they're fascinating."

"Harry, I can introduce you to lots of them in the French Quarter."

"The French Quarter was a hangout for pirates in the 1800's. Did you know that in a few days Key West will be packed with tourists for Pirate Fest?"

"Wow! I had no idea. What is that?"

"It's like everything pirates. This is the first year. When Pirate Week in November became successful the City Council decided to start a two week Pirate Fest in the spring. They're even going to have a famous pirate lookalike contest."

"I bet my Grandfather would love to go. Everyone tells him he looks just like Jean Lafitte."

"Let's hope you don't find what you're looking for too soon. I'd like to show you Pirate Fest."

"I would like that." Their eyes met. She could feel the connection that had been made.

A flight attendant, coming down the aisle, was pushing a cart filled with drinks and snacks. Amy caught her eye in time before she got to Jimmy's seat. She whispered to the flight attendant, "My friend, behind us, aisle seat, needs his sleep. Please don't wake him."

The pretty young girl took one look at Jimmy snoring peacefully and got the message. She whispered. "No problem."

Amy looked at Harry and blushed.

Harry smiled. "Amy Lafitte, I want to know everything about you."

"Where do I start?"

"At the beginning."

Amy looked him in the eye and smiled. "I'm a simple country girl, recently moved to New Orleans to be with my family and now I'm just taking life easy."

Harry grinned. "There is nothing simple about you."

"Tell me about your life. Did you always know you wanted to fly? I really admire someone who knows what they want to do at a young age."

"Did you?"

"Not really."

At that moment the intercom crackled into an announcement stating their arrival into Miami International.

"We'll continue this conversation later." Harry put his tray table up.

The landing was smooth.

Jimmy woke up grumbling and asking when snacks were going to be served. He disappeared for a second looking for emergency rations in his backpack under his seat.

Amy laughed. Some things never change.

As they walked through the terminal Amy introduced Harry and brought Jimmy up to date about Pirate Fest. She told him that Harry had offered to drive them from Miami to Key West and then take them to the island in his boat."

"What kind of boat do you have?" Jimmy slipped his backpack from his shoulder to his back.

"A sailboat."

"Is it big?"

"Big enough."

"And does it have engines in case the wind dies down?"

"It does."

"Good thing because I can't swim."

"Jimmy, you didn't tell me you can't swim." She thought just about everyone living near water knew how to swim and the French Quarter was right over the levee from the Mississippi River. She had taught herself to swim in the small indoor pool in the orphanage basement.

"You didn't ask."

"Make sure you wear your life jacket at all times." Amy thought about the hard time she had getting him to wear the bike helmet.

Amy couldn't see the big grin on his face. He was sure Harry didn't have a small life jacket on his boat.

Like he was reading Jimmy's thoughts Harry looked at Amy and grinned, "Not to worry I keep water wings in case my Dad has a client with kids."

Jimmy struggled not to make a scene about water wings for babies. How embarrassing! There was no way he'd wear them. Just try and make him!

Since they all had carryon bags they went right out to the curb.

"No luggage?" Amy asked.

"Nope. Just a backpack. I travel light."

They had just exited the terminal when a sleek black limo drove up.

"Hey, Joey." Harry greeted the driver who quickly stowed Amy's bag in the trunk.

"Hope you haven't been waiting long. Traffic was brutal." The driver was young and dressed in jeans and a t-shirt. "Two days ago your Dad flew some buyers to Key West. He picked up his boat and took them to the Bahamas to do some fishing. He said to tell you he'll be gone for about a week."

"That sounds like my Dad. I'm headed for Key West myself."

Harry introduced Amy and Jimmy.

While Joey walked around to the driver's side Harry got in back with Amy and Jimmy. He explained that his Dad usually sent the limo for Lear Jet buyers.

Jimmy, quiet until now, joined the conversation. "I've never been in a limo before."

"You have too! Remember the limo that took us to the Ball?"

"Oh, the one where the driver tried to kidnap us until Serena turned him into a Cajun rat?"

Amy put a hand over her eyes. Wasn't there anything he could keep to himself!

"Oh, I know you're just dying to tell me that story." Harry had an amused smile on his face.

"Oh, yes." Amy gave him a grim smile and looked out the window, wondering what he would do if he knew the truth about her family. Probably look for an exit door, she thought.

Harry laughed. "Anyway, as far as I know Joey hasn't kidnapped anyone." He picked up the phone by his right side. "Joey, drop us at my house."

Jimmy made himself comfortable. "Anything to eat?"

"On our way down the Keys I know a great place."

"It's open on Sunday?"

Harry laughed. "Everything is open on Sunday. The Keyes are packed with tourists on the weekend."

"Is this great place very far from Miami?" Jimmy, sitting across from Harry and Amy, asked sweetly.

Amy looked right at Jimmy and narrowed her eyes. "I always thought it's the place that counts not how fast you can get to the food, Jimmy!" She gave him such an evil eye he quickly turned and looked out the window.

"Oh, I agree one hundred percent." He called over his shoulder. He got the message. He continued to complain but in a whisper.

Harry pointed out the sights of Miami. Jimmy had a lot of questions. He'd never been to Miami before, and since he'd been just about everywhere else in the whole world, this was a big adventure.

Soon they turned off the main road and sped down a tree lined driveway. Amy caught glimpses of blue water through the trees. The limo pulled up to a cozy beach bungalow. It was a one story made of weathered white wood siding with a red clay tile roof. After retrieving Amy's small valise from the trunk Joey wasted no time in taking off.

Harry pulled a car cover off a faded red '65 Mustang Convertible. He lifted the trunk and deposited his backpack inside.

"Cool car, Harry." Jimmy loved American classic cars.

"Thanks. Listen I have to collect a few things. I'll be quick. Want to come inside? You can leave your things in the car." Jimmy threw his backpack into the back seat. Amy put her valise in the trunk and made a mental note to get a backpack as soon as possible.

Harry retrieved his door key hidden in the dirt of a half barrel of Thyme. The smell was lovely as Amy passed the fragrant herb on the way through the door. The entry was small with hooks on the wall for coats. There was a small kitchen on the right that opened into a large living room.

"Help yourself." There are cold drinks in the fridge." Harry called out as he picked up a briefcase and started filling it with papers from his desk.

Jimmy headed for the kitchen. "Can I make a cheese sandwich? I'm starved." Jimmy called from the open door of the refrigerator.

"Sure. Help yourself."

"Harry, this is really lovely." Amy stood looking out the French doors in the living room. There was a charming brick courtyard that opened to a small green grass yard leading to a long concrete dock extending out into the water.

"When I have time I love to fish off the dock." He stood beside her. Her hair smelled so good. "Sometimes I bring my boat here. But the fishing is much better in the Keys."

"I can imagine sitting on that brick patio and reading a book."

"I love to read, too."

Jimmy joined them with a cheese sandwich wrapped in paper towels. He smiled. "Amy read just about every book in the library at the orphanage."

Harry looked at Amy in surprise. "Orphanage?"

"Mmm." Amy knew that wasn't an answer. She gave Jimmy the evil eye. *Jimmy O'Brien, when are you going to shut up? I'll tell Harry myself about the orphanage and anything else about myself that I want to tell him. I don't need a blabby autobiographer running around behind me!!!*

Ohhhh, aren't we just Miss Grumpy!!!! Turning his attention to Harry he asked. "How long is the drive to Key West?"

"Just a few hours. It really depends on the traffic. Ready?"

"Let's go."

It was a perfect Miami afternoon for the top down. Jimmy climbed into the back seat. After finishing his sandwich he fell asleep.

Harry laughed. "Does he sleep at night?"

"I have no idea."

"You are such a mystery."

As they drove down the Keys she told him she had returned to New Orleans this past January, a few weeks before Mardi Gras. She told him about the Pirates Ball, the call outs and how exciting it was to be part of it. There was a lot she didn't say like she didn't mention the curse. She really liked how Harry didn't push her. When she was ready she'd talk to him but for right now she wasn't ready.

Harry was fascinated with Amy. He had never met a woman who was so strong and resilient. But if he wanted to get to know her he would have to take it slow. He knew she wasn't someone who trusted easily.

"Tell me about yourself? I know you grew up in Massachusetts. You're home based in Miami and fly planes to buyers for your Dad's company Morgan Air. I'd love to hear all the parts you didn't tell me."

"Are you hungry?"

Amy had not eaten anything since breakfast. "Yes!"

He laughed. "I love a woman with an appetite. I know a place with terrific hamburgers. And a seafood platter, too."

"You mean both are in one place?"

"The best I've ever had."

"Wow! Let's go there."

Harry smiled at her, a woman who was not high maintenance. He wanted to get to know her better, much better.

With the top down and Jimmy snoring in the backseat it was hard to keep up a conversation. Amy finally leaned her head back, closed her eyes and enjoyed the warm wind whipping her hair about her face.

The time went by so fast it felt like they had just left Miami when Harry was pulling off the highway onto a crushed shell driveway towards a seaside shack with the lettering "Buck's Burger and Clams" over the front door.

Jimmy woke up just in time to help Harry put the top up on the car.

The hamburger joint looked like any one of many beach hangouts but the inside looked like the 50's. There was a long counter with red vinyl stools or if you were lucky you might find a red vinyl booth next to a floor to ceiling picture window that looked out at water foaming over a white sandy beach. It was breathtaking.

"Let's sit at the counter." Amy loved the smell of the sizzling burgers.

The cook turned to see his new guests. "Burgers, Harry?"

Amy nodded enthusiastically. Jimmy did, too. Burgers were his favorite.

"New friends?"

"Buck, this is Amy and Jimmy."

"Hi, Buck. The hamburgers look great!" Amy loved the food in America. She had spent thirteen years at the orphanage eating

Irish and Scottish fare which was good, but it didn't include burgers and onion rings.

Jimmy went over to the jute box. He selected an oldie from The Platters album. He made it back to the table just in time to see Buck placing a large platter of onion rings in front of Amy along with a steaming hot burger on a soft sesame seed bun. "From now on, don't be a stranger, Miss Amy. You too, Jimmy."

"She's from New Orleans but I hope to talk her into coming here...now and then." Harry smiled at Amy.

"I might." She laughed. She took a portion of the onion rings and passed the rest down the counter. The minute she picked up her burger all talk stopped. This was the seriously best hamburger ever.

Jimmy looked like he loved everything!

By the time they finished a storm cloud had turned the sky charcoal grey. Buck flipped on the lights.

Amy figured they were leaving just in time when a crack of thunder and a flash of lightening lit up the dark sky. "I'm glad you put the top up."

The first fat raindrops fell just as Jimmy got to the car first and dove into the back seat. Harry saw Amy in and shut the door before running around to his side.

"It was sunny when we left Miami." Jimmy grumbled.

"This is Florida. We get sudden storms all the time."

Amy looked at Jimmy, a backpack under his head, and now stretched out on the back seat. "Jimmy, are you okay?"

"I'm fine. Aunt Maggie left two nights ago and we all had to stay up until three in the morning. She didn't want anyone to see her flying off on her carpet."

"A flying carpet?" Harry didn't know whether to be amazed or amused.

"A figure of speech." Amy quickly added. She had to remind Jimmy again to watch what he said...at least for now.

"Then last night I stayed up all night organizing my brothers on what to do and how to take care of everything until I got back. I just didn't get any sleep."

"I understand. Anyway we're not that far from Key West. The refrigerator in the cottage is stocked in case you need anything."

"A cottage?" She had not been looking forward to a busy hotel.

"Morgan Air keeps a place in Key West for potential buyers to stay. I have the key. You and Jimmy stay there. I'll crash on my boat. Pirate Fest starts in a few days so all the hotels are booked and they're really noisy anyway. The cottage is right on the beach so you can hear the waves at night."

"Thank you, Harry." Amy was touched by his thoughtfulness. "Could we stop at the Police Station first? I want to see if they have anything new on Bugs and let them know we're here."

"Sure. I'll give Chief Barker a call."

Amy went over all her notes on Bugs, preparing to ask questions while Harry called on his cell phone. The conversation was quick. The police chief assured Harry he would wait for them.

They finally pulled up in front of a light grey concrete building. Dark green shutters flanked every window in the large four story building. The police station was definitely hurricane protected. Amy glanced up through the windshield to the top floor and noted the heavy bars.

Harry saw her looking up. "That's the city jail."

Amy smiled. "With a water view. Can't be all bad."

Jimmy woke up when Harry parked. He followed them into the police station. "Hey, what's up, guys! Jimmy was surprised to see his pirate friends, One Eye and Jocko, from Treasure Island leaning on the counter and talking to one of the officers.

"Well, I'll be, our poker buddy!" They patted Jimmy on the back.

"Hey, Harry, you know Amy?" They bowed in fun. "Or should we say Pirate Queen Amy!"

Harry could see into the Chief's glass office. He was on the phone. "Pirate Queen Amy?" He gave her an inquiring look.

"Amy was Queen of the Pirates Ball at Mardi Gras this year. The most beautiful Pirate Queen ever."

Harry laughed and shook hands with them. "How are you guys doing? You're here for Pirate Fest, I bet."

"Much to our surprise we've been asked to run the whole show."

"Fantastic! Are we going to have our poker games, too?" Jimmy was thrilled at the idea.

"Of course!" Jocko and One Eye looked at each other and silently decided something. "Amy, we want you to be our Pirate Queen and lead the Pirate Fest parade. All you do is wear a lady pirate captain's costume on the first lead float and throw doubloons, ropes of pearls and pirate themed beads to the crowd. It's like a pirate Mardi Gras. You will be the Pirate Queen and ride on the lead float with the Pirate King."

"Who will be the Pirate King?"

"Didn't Harry tell you? It's the pirate who wins the Jean Lafitte Pirate lookalike contest this year. So, what do you say?"

"Wow! Thanks! That sounds like a lot of fun. Doesn't Pirate Fest start in a few days?"

"It does. On Friday. I know this is short notice but if you can't ride the float just let Chief Barker know. He'll get a message to us. In which case I'll either stick a wig on Jocko and squeeze him into a Pirate Queen gown or we'll have to have the first Pirate King alone up there! Pirate Amy is my choice."

Amy started laughing at the thought of big manly Jocko riding the float as a Pirate Queen. "I don't know yet but I promise to do my best to make it. But first we have to wrap up a case. Did you know Jimmy and I started a Detective Agency?"

"We heard. What is this case you're on?"

"Our first clients came to us to find their nephew, Bugs Robichaux. He inherited Castle Island. It's located somewhere off Key West. He sent them a postcard saying he arrived, sold the island and then disappeared."

"Castle Island. That's in the middle of the Bermuda Triangle." Jocko looked a bit worried.

"We know."

"You know Serena and Jean is coming to Pirate Fest."

"She didn't tell me."

"How could she not with a Jean Lafitte pirate lookalike contest."

Amy laughed. "That's fantastic."

Harry leaned close to Amy and whispered, "I can't wait to hear about Pirate Queen Amy. You are fascinating!"

"How are you getting out to Castle Island? Do you need a ride? I hear Blackbeard and his Queen Anne's Revenge is going to be here."

"Thanks, Jocko, but Harry offered to take us in his boat. But Blackbeard! Wow! Did you know that Harry is related to Blackbeard?"

"Really! I had no idea, Harry, you old pirate. You'll be right at home with all the other pirates."

"This is going to be a lot of fun." Amy wondered if Jocko meant the real Blackbeard was going to be here. She would soon find out.

One Eye laughed. "Yes, it is. I heard Jean talked Serena into coming so he could enter the pirate lookalike contest."

"Oh, I had no idea! Let me know about Blackbeard, okay!" Serena had been talking about inviting him for dinner sometime.

Jocko turned to Harry. You're taking out the **Gone Fishin?** Whoa! That hunk of rust hasn't sunk yet, Harry?" "Not yet." Harry smiled.

The Chief stuck his head out of his office and waved Harry to come in. "Ready?"

Jocko waved to Amy. "We have to go. See you at Pirate Fest." Before they left they waved to Jimmy who had discovered a small freezer in the corner with Lime Ice Box Pie Popsicles.

"Jimmy, are you coming or not?" Amy did not look happy.

Harry shook hands with a tall, handsome man wearing a baseball cap with fly fishing lures secured on each side of the hat. "Chief Barker, Amy Lafitte and Jimmy O'Brien, private detectives from New Orleans. They're looking for their client's missing nephew."

"Sit down." He indicated chairs in front of his well-worn wood desk. Amy liked the police chief. He had salt and pepper hair and looked somewhere in his fifties. He was in great shape, too. "What do you have?"

"Two sisters, Lynne and Gayle Robichaux, hired us a few days ago. Their nephew inherited Castle Island off Key West. His name is Bugs Robichaux. They got a postcard when he arrived and then one saying he'd sold Castle Island and then nothing."

The Chief leaned back in his desk chair and pulled out a file from a cabinet behind him. He quickly scanned the information.

"You know they filed a missing person report when they didn't hear from Bugs."

"I didn't know that. They didn't say they talked to you."

"They came here in person looking for him. I went out to Castle Island and spoke to the new owners. Bugs Robichaux sold the island, and the castle on the fifty acre island, to Reverend Damian and his wife Madame Sonya. They paid Bugs two million dollars."

"Two million dollars?" Amy was surprised.

"In cash. Waterfront property is out of sight. The Reverend showed me a bill of sale and it was witnessed by two of our most distinguished Key West residents, Marty and Martha Perkins. I interviewed the Perkins and it was all done legally. Marty is a Notary and a retired, well known Attorney."

"The sisters didn't tell us any of this."

"Well if they hired you maybe they didn't want to influence your investigation. I explained to the sisters that he rented a boat from Grayson and after Bugs left the island he disappeared along with the boat and the cash. It's not the first boat that's disappeared in that area. Castle Island is in the middle of the Bermuda Triangle and strange things have happened there."

87

I'd like to talk to Mr. & Mrs. Perkins, also Grayson who rented the boat to Bugs, and I want to go out to Castle Island myself and talk to the Reverend and his wife."

"Let me know if you find out anything new." The Chief waved to a desk officer who took the file from him and left the office. "Officer Boomer is going to copy the file and give you everything I have on Bugs. All the phone numbers and addresses are in there." The Chief shook hands with Amy and Jimmy. "Good luck."

"Thank you, Chief Barker. We'll be in touch."

The Chief patted Harry on the back. "Harry, good to see you. You'll be here for Pirate Fest, right?"

"I wouldn't miss it." Harry followed Amy and Jimmy into the outer office where they waited for the files to be copied. He noticed that Amy hadn't said anything about a map and pirate treasure to the Chief. He figured she had her reasons.

Amy used Harry's cell phone to call the phone numbers provided by the Police Chief. No one answered. Grayson's message machine said office hours were seven in the morning until four in the afternoon. Mr. & Mrs. Perkins had an answering service that picked up their calls and advised them to call back the next day after nine in the morning. They discreetly did not say whether they were in or out that evening. Amy purposefully didn't call Reverend Damian on

Castle Island. She explained to Harry that she would learn more from a surprise visit.

She handed him his phone. "No one home anywhere. I think we'll start early tomorrow."

"I'll drop you and Jimmy off. I have work to do at the Marina getting my boat ready. Is seven too early? I know a terrific place for breakfast before we get started with your list."

"Thanks, Harry. We'll be ready."

Detective Boomer handed them the files and they left the building.

Driving to a rural area, with a stretch of quiet beach outside of Key West proper, Harry pulled up in front of a Caribbean style house, painted in colors of white with salmon trim and dark blue shutters on all the windows, with a dark blue front door.

"We're here."

"It's so pretty." Amy loved the cozy island feel to the one story cottage. A turnaround in front had a palm tree in the middle. Giant ferns and coconut trees were scattered all over the one acre.

"There's a patio off the living room that goes down to the water. You have a lot of privacy here. The nearest neighbor is a distance away and they're hardly ever there anyway. There are four bedrooms to choose from."

"It's quiet. I need that right now." Amy smiled at Harry.

Jimmy jumped out and retrieved Amy's small bag from the trunk. Remembering the stocked refrigerator he was eager to get inside.

Harry came around and opened Amy's door. She really loved his gentlemanly southern gestures.

"See you at seven." Amy hoped he couldn't see her blushing.

"I look forward to it." And did he ever! She was like the perfect woman: a great sense of humor, interesting, very smart, really beautiful, very easy to talk to, and loved hamburgers over caviar! Wow!

He walked her to the front door, opened it, handed her the key then he drove off. He was glad Jimmy was with her for protection.

When he got to the Key West Marina country store, where he usually stocked up on food and supplies, it was closed for the night. He'd talk to the owner, Paulo, in the morning. Harry took in the sight of his boat gently rolling with the waves caused by other boats coming to dock for the night. He took a quick shower, ate a peanut butter and banana sandwich, and got into the lower bunk. He turned on a fan and pushed open a porthole near his head and one by his feet. The cross ventilation was fantastic! He liked to count the roll of the waves. By the time he reached ten he was sound asleep.

Amy was still keyed up. She opened a sliding door and sat on a patio chair listening to the waves hit the sandy beach. The sound was soft but still loud enough to be heard from the house.

She heard the refrigerator door open and shut. Smiling she slid open the patio door to the living room. "Come join me."

"Want anything to eat?" "Nope."

"Be right there."

Jimmy sat down in a lounge chair next to Amy and made short work of what looked like a scoop of ice cream covered in chocolate syrup and a slice of frozen pound cake.

How does he eat like that and not gain weight? Amy wondered silently.

Jimmy grumbled. "I get a lot of exercise. I take two steps to your one."

"It's really beautiful here, isn't it?"

"Yes."

"Jimmy..."

"Yes."

"You are my very dearest friend and always will be. No one will ever come between our friendship, at least not on my part."

"I know."

"Harry is the first guy I've met that's my age. In the orphanage I was the oldest by far. And there were no guys like Harry around anyway."

"I know. I'm sorry I've acted a bit rotten at times."

"I'm just getting to know Harry. He really seems like a great guy."

"It takes time to get to know someone."

"Okay, Dad!" Amy smiled. "I'm glad we had this talk."
"Me too."

"I'm going to sleep. See you in the morning. I noticed there was an alarm clock by my bed. You must have one, too."

"I don't know. I'm going to stay up for a bit."

Amy got up. "Good thing you slept most of the day." Amy took a quick shower, set her alarm and climbed into bed. She fell asleep clicking off a list of things to do.

CHAPTER FOUR

Amy promises to find Frankie

Harry was up early. Buck's hamburger, yesterday afternoon, was the last meal he'd had, except for the PB and banana sandwich last night. He needed a big breakfast very soon. For the first time he picked what he wanted to wear. Usually jeans a t-shirt and his leather flight jacket was like a uniform. Today he put on white pants, a navy blue shirt, dark brown leather deck shoes, and a navy blue wool L.L. Bean jacket.

Amy was up and dressed. She knocked on Jimmy's door and yelled for him to get going.

She was sitting on the patio, having a cup of coffee, when Harry arrived.

"Hey, I'm ready. I'm not sure about Jimmy. He was still primping an hour ago."

"I heard that!" Jimmy shouted from the bedroom.

"No rush." Harry knew Grayson doesn't keep regular hours. "His phone number is probably in the file you were given. Why don't you call him about the boat he rented to Bugs? He has a place in the Marina."

"Good idea."

"I thought I'd make us some breakfast, instead of going out, if you like."

"I do." Hmm, Amy thought, a man who can cook. Good thing because it wasn't her strong point.

Amy used Harry's cell phone while he was busy in the kitchen and from the wonderful smell bacon was sizzling in the pan and eggs were frying.

Grayson answered his phone right away. "Grayson Rentals."

"Mr. Grayson. My name is Amy Lafitte. I'm looking for Bugs Robichaux. He rented a boat from you about a year ago." "I ran into Chief Barker last night and he mentioned you would be calling."

"As it turns out I'll be coming to the Marina in a short while. Do you mind if I stop in for a chat?"

"I don't mind at all. I love chatting up pretty young ladies!"

Amy smiled. Grayson sounded like he was in his eighties.

"Where are you located?"

"I'm right next to the public boat launch. I figured it was a good spot. People come down for a day of fishing, get their boat in the water and then it won't run. They look around and spot my sign...Grayson Boats for Rent. I get a lot of business like that."

Amy laughed. "I bet you do. Okay see you soon." She liked talking to someone in person rather than by phone. Not all the time, but sometimes, you can read a person better face to face.

Grayson checked a wall clock that had been hanging over the door about as long as he had been in business. "I just remembered. I have an errand to run. I'll be back by ten."

"Okay, see you later."

She called Marty and Martha Perkins, the couple who witnessed the sale of Castle Island. She hoped she could see them first. The phone rang twice.

"Perkin residence."

"I'm looking for Mr. or Mrs. Perkins."

"They not here! Dios Mio! Everybody looking for Senor Marty. I only housekeeper. They leave una nota. No back for dos or tres dias! They go to Bahamas in their boat."

"Where do they keep the boat...at the Marina?"

"Si, at Marina. I not know where...only name of boat. Un momento!" The line went dead for a few seconds. "You there, Senora."

"Si, I'm here!"

"The MaryLou. That name...the MaryLou."

"Thank you."

"You leave phone number?" "No. I'll call later if I miss them."

Jimmy was in the kitchen talking to Harry when Amy returned his cell phone. Egg and bacon sandwiches were on the table with a pot of hot coffee.

"Okay. Here's the latest. Grayson said he'd talk to me when I got to the Marina, but not before ten, and Marty and Martha Perkins are taking their boat to the Bahamas today. Their housekeeper said they had just left for the Marina. I have to talk to the Perkins' before they leave.

Harry dialed the Marina Store. From what Paulo said the couple had just arrived but had some repairs to take care of before leaving so he asked Paulo to tell them someone who wanted to talk to them was on their way.

"You have time. They aren't going anywhere for a few hours." Paulo said before hanging up.

Harry relayed the information to Amy.

It was the best egg and bacon sandwich Amy had ever had. Jimmy ate with his usual big appetite but he looked tired.

"Jimmy, you look exhausted." Amy was worried about her friend.

"I can't sleep without chaos around me." He explained to Harry. "I have three younger brothers who are incredibly busy all the time. I called home last night. They were playing the game."

"The game?" Harry was amused. He was an only child so it was hard to imagine being around three active younger brothers.

Amy smiled. "It's a board game called "The Pirates Treasure Game. It's really big in Pirates village."

"Where is Pirates Village? I've never heard of it."

"It's in the French Quarter. If you come to visit I'll show you."

"I will."

Their eyes met. Amy felt a little thrill. It was something she'd never felt before and it was a wonderful feeling.

Jimmy rolled his eyes and ate two more sandwiches. They finished and were at the Marina in a short time.

This was another first in Amy's life. Key West Marina was one long dock after another with space for everything from a canoe to a hundred foot yacht. Harry's boat fell somewhere in between. There were two Morgan boats spaces. The larger of the two was vacant. Amy remembered the driver who picked them up told Harry that his Dad had taken his boat to the Bahamas. Amy noticed the two tie lines were about one hundred feet apart. Big boat...I think they call that a yacht!

Harry's boat was across the walkway on the other side of the dock. It was a sleek, gleaming white beauty. Amy laughed when she thought about One Eye teasing Harry about a hunk of rust. She noticed it was called *"Gone Fishing."*

Jimmy was busy checking out the sails so Amy followed Harry. There were bunks right and left of the stairs with privacy curtains that could be pulled shut. The stairs ended in the main lounge. A large leather sofa, that could easily seat six, was across from the galley.

Harry started pointing out things for her. "That's the galley. It's small but has everything I need. The head is on the left. Again small but complete. Across is a pantry for supplies. The closed door at the end is a stateroom with---"

"I know." Amy added. "Everything you need. Maybe even a TV."

"How did you know that?" He smiled. "I think you're psychic."

"Might be. Also I noticed you have a BBQ grill leaning against the bench seat outside. I bet you cook the fish you catch."

"You guess right. Frying fish in a small cabin smells great only for the first few minutes."

Amy went to check out the bedroom. Harry looked around. He was proud of his boat. Usually it was messy but it was home when he stayed in Key West, which was most of the time, except when his Dad had a plane for him to deliver. Knowing he was bringing Amy back here he had changed the linens and cleaned the kitchen. His Dad taught him to fly when he was ten years old so he had a license to fly just about anything, from helos to props to jets, from visual only to computer radar.

Jimmy clattered down the stairs. Amy joined them.

"Jimmy, you and I take the bunk beds. Amy you take the bedroom."

"I feel like a Queen."

"Oh yeah, we need to talk about that, Pirate Queen Amy."

"Ah, yes. And we will have time." Amy had no idea how she would tell him about her family but right now she had work to do. "Jimmy, do you want to come? I have to talk to Grayson and Mr. & Mrs. Perkins."

He really didn't so he dragged it out. "Well..."

"If you want...hang out with Harry and I'll be back."

Jimmy was grateful and so was Amy. She had a feeling Grayson was a man who would easily talk to her but not so easy if she was there with a male someone else.

"Wow, thanks, Amy."

From the top deck Harry pointed to a huge yacht. "The Perkins boat, the MaryLou is docked two piers over." Harry waved and disappeared into the main cabin with Jimmy right behind him. She headed first to talk to Mr. and Mrs. Perkins before they took off. Grayson had told her he wouldn't be back until ten.

The Perkins boat was a fifty foot sailboat with a teak deck and dark green seat cushions. Pristine white sails were loosely tied, waiting for the yacht to leave the harbor. A bilge pump was furiously at work pumping water out an opening on the side.

A young man, dressed all in white with a jaunty Captain's hat on his head, tilted to one side, was just stepping off the walkway from the dock to the deck of the yacht. He turned when he heard someone approaching, "Hello, can I help you?"

"I would like to speak to Mr. or Mrs. Perkins."

"Just a minute." He disappeared into the cabin. Amy was grateful she had worn tennis shoes today.

A woman, who looked to be in her early sixties, in excellent shape, appeared from below. "Well, hello there. I'm Martha Perkins. Can I help you?"

"I hope so. I'm Amy Lafitte from New Orleans. I'm trying to find some information on Bugs Robichaux. I was told that about a year ago he sold Castle Island, and you and your husband witnessed the transaction."

"Yes. We did. Please come aboard."

Amy took the walkway to the boat like she'd been boarding yachts all her life when really, until now, the only boat she had been on was the small ferry Seamus used to bring mail and visitors to the orphanage. She followed Mrs. Perkins into a large room filled with overstuffed chairs upholstered in light blue silk brocade. Everything moveable was bolted to the floor. Lacey curtains at the windows gave the look of a lovely sitting room rather than a lounge on a yacht exposed to wind and salt water spray.

"Can I offer you something...coffee...tea?"

"Coffee would be nice. Thank you."

Mrs. Perkins spoke into an intercom on the end table next to the sofa. "Ed, would you bring coffee for two and those little cakes."

She turned back to Amy. "I remember Bugs. A very nice young man. I take it if you're asking about him he hasn't been found yet."

Amy shook her head.

Mrs. Perkins continued, "As I told the Police Chief, and also his two aunts who came here from New Orleans, we were visiting the Castle at the time. Reverend Damian asked us to witness the signing of a legal bill of sale. My husband is an attorney and a notary. Later that day we left for the mainland. We had to be home for a charity event later that evening."

Amy showed her the picture she had of Bugs.

Mrs. Perkins took the picture and carefully looked at it. "That's him, all right. A really sweet young man and very happy with the sale."

"You said you visited the Castle?"

"Why yes. It's a magnificent place. The Reverend is renowned for his abilities."

"What is it that he does?"

"He speaks to the dead. His wife, Madame Sonya, holds séances once a month and also reads Tarot cards. Have you had your cards read?"

"No."

"If you visit there you must."

"And you were there...."

The older woman had been trying to avoid talking about their reasons for seeking the counsel of Reverend Damian. "We had recently lost our daughter. It was a terrible time. Someone told us about the Reverend. I convinced my husband to take me to Castle Island. The Reverend was very compassionate. The first night we were there he held a séance and MaryLou spoke to us. She said she was in a wonderful place, not to ever worry about her again." Her eyes welled with tears. "At the time I...I didn't want to leave. The Reverend asked us to witness the sale of the island. How could we refuse him? It was handled with correct legal procedure. My husband is an attorney and also a notary. After the sale the Reverend opened a bottle of champagne. We toasted the sale and then we left for the mainland. I remember Reverend Damian paid Bugs in cash. Two million dollars. Bugs seemed incredibly happy. He said he was leaving for Key West later that day. We only heard from the police when his two aunts, from New Orleans, arrived in Key West looking for him. They came to our house in town. We told them everything we knew, which was unfortunately not very much. We have had no contact with the Reverend, or his wife, since that day."

"Mrs. Perkins, if you don't mind my asking, why have you not had any further contact with them?"

"After we returned home we heard some unsavory things about the Reverend and his wife from a few of our friends. We decided not to be involved with Reverend Damian or his wife. They tried calling us a few time."

"They wanted you to return and visit?"

"Yes, but my husband didn't want to go back. He thinks there is something dark that surrounds the Reverend and his wife. Even his wife called trying to get us to come back but we said no. Anyway, we assumed at the time, that the young man returned home or sailed around the world."

"Sailed around the world?"

"Right before we left the island, the Reverend came to see us off and told us the young man said he might buy a sailboat and go around the world."

"I see."

"If you can wait my husband will be back shortly."

"I'm sorry I can't stay. Thank you for talking to me."

"Of course. I hope you find that young man."

"I will."

Amy knew Mrs. Perkins was telling the truth. She detected nothing deceptive from what she had just said. She wondered why the sisters hadn't told her about their visit to the couple but then it was like their visit to the Police Chief, which they also hadn't mentioned, they probably wanted her to see it without a preconceived idea of what they had discovered.

Amy walked away from that meeting very relieved. She was sure Mrs. Perkins and her husband were not friends with the Reverend. She was sure they wouldn't call and tell him of her visit. She wanted to meet him without his having any advanced warning.

She had no trouble finding *Grayson Boat Rentals.* The office was right where he said it was, next to the public boat launch. Mr. Grayson was on the phone so Amy waited on the screened porch. She didn't have to wait long.

"Come on in, young lady." Grayson called from inside.

Amy went in and sat down. Everything was dingy, gray and rundown. Grayson was busy fiddling with something under his desk, which looked like a catch-all wood table heaped to overflowing with empty beer cans and files.

"This is how you stop the calls...unplug the phone!" He popped up. "What can I do for you? I'm booked from yesterday until two weeks after Pirate Fest. I hope you are not looking for a boat."

"I'm not. I'm looking for Bugs Robichaux. He rented one of your boats about a year ago." Amy handed him the picture of Bugs she had in her pocket.

Grayson studied the picture carefully. "Yep. I can't forget someone who disappeared with my *Maybeline.*" Seeing her perplexing stare he hastened to add. "That was the name of my boat. I told Chief Barker I had no idea where he was at the time. I just know he wasn't back at my dock on the day his rental was up. My

Maybeline was a seaworthy vessel, that's for sure. He might be in the Caribbean for all I know. If you find him get my boat back. He was sailing right into the Bermuda Triangle. Not the safest place even on a good day. He said he had inherited an island."

Amy added. "He did and then he sold the island to a Reverend Damian."

Grayson whistled. "I bet Mr. Robichaux made a pretty penny on that deal." Leaning back in his chair he grabbed two cans of Tecate beer out of an apartment size refrigerator. He popped the top on one and took a long drink. "Dry throat!" He grinned and indicated the other can was for Amy who declined his offer.

She watched the frosty can drip water that slid down the sides and formed a small puddle on the top of his desk. The water ring joined all the other stains on the fading wood finish.

"Mr. Grayson, from what I know he's not the kind of young man to take off and not come back but if I find the boat I'll certainly get it back to you."

"Maybelline...Maybelline in black letters across the stern." He started to mumble.

Amy handed him a business card. "Here's my name and phone number in case Bugs comes back." This was something she really didn't see happening but she was sure he was still alive.

Dropping the card into the top drawer of his desk he finished his beer and did a perfect shot into a trash can across the room.

Amy picked up Bug's picture and put it in her bag. She hoped Mr. Grayson would remember Bugs if he saw him again.

On her way back to the dock she saw Harry going into the Marina store.

Harry turned when Amy walked in. "Amy, this is Paulo Garcia. He runs the store and he's a first class boat mechanic."

Amy thought he looked a lot like the actor, Andy Garcia.

"Any news about Frankie?" Harry asked Paulo.
"None."

Shaking off his grief he gave her a big smile. "Hi Amy. Welcome to Key West. You came at a good time. We are going to have the first Pirate Fest."

"Amy is a private detective from New Orleans. Her partner, Jimmy, came in here earlier. They're looking for Bugs Robichaux. He inherited Castle Island. About a year ago he came here looking for the island. He rented a boat from Grayson but then he disappeared."

Amy took out the one photo she had of Bugs and showed it to Paulo. "Have you seen him?"

Paulo studied the photo. "I never forget a face. He stopped here for supplies. Quiet, didn't say much. In a hurry. That's all I remember. A few months later the police brought two elderly ladies to the Marina. They were looking for him. I told them everything I knew, which wasn't much. I only saw him that one time."

"Thanks, Paulo."

"Do you want me to photocopy his picture? You can put it up in shop windows. I'm putting one up right now."

Paulo walked over to the front of the store and taped a missing poster to the front window. Amy picked up one of the posters on the counter. "What a lovely girl. Who is Frankie?"

"My sister, Francesca. Everyone calls her Frankie. Six months ago she disappeared on her way home from work."

"I saw a large poster with missing persons at the police station but I didn't see anyone who looked like Frankie."

"That's because I didn't go to the police."

"You didn't file a missing persons report?"

Paulo looked down. He wished he could have reported her missing but he couldn't. "Frankie is here illegally."

"But you're here."

"I married a girl from Key West. I'm a legal resident."

"I'll take some of the posters. You never know."

Harry returned to the counter with a canvas tote filled with supplies. "Call me if my boat parts come in. I want to get going as fast as possible."

Paulo rang up his provisions.

Harry smiled at Amy. "Jimmy is waiting on the boat in case the delivery gets there first. Do you think he would like some snacks? Waiting around to fix a boat is the boring part of sailing."

"Thanks. He would really love that."

While Paulo rang up his provisions Amy grabbed all the snacks she thought Jimmy would like.

Harry caught her eye. "See you later." She watched him walk out the door with his arms full of groceries. She turned back to Paulo. "Tell me about Frankie."

"She came to Key West because I was here. Our Mom went to California for medical treatments. I send her everything I make each month but it was nowhere enough for her medical bills. Frankie got a job in housekeeping at The Blue Dolphin, a local hotel. The day she disappeared she told us she that morning that she had a possible new job. She said she would be making a lot more money. She wouldn't tell us anything. Frankie said it was bad luck to talk about possible good fortune in advance and, she said, they hired her on a two week probation. If it didn't work out she'd be back."

"Where did she live? Did she have an apartment with roommates?"

"Frankie lived with us. Apartments are expensive in Key West. We were lucky. This job came with a large two bedroom apartment upstairs. Frankie shared a room with our twin boys."

Amy looked at Paulo. He was close to tears. She sensed that after Frankie disappeared he didn't know what to do. Sometimes when you don't know what to do you do nothing hoping everything will work out. It rarely does. "Do you mind if I look into it? I want to help you find her. There's no charge."

Paulo stood a little taller. A smile of hope lit up his eyes. When she had first walked into the store he looked like a man defeated. He didn't look like that anymore. "Amy, I don't know how to thank you. I don't have a lot but I would give anything to find Frankie. I love my sister. I know she's not dead. I just know it. I won't give up."

Amy could feel that Frankie was alive somewhere.

Paul ran off a stack of pictures of Bugs and handed them to her. "I remember talking to him when he came in and stocked up on supplies. We talked about the weather, things in general. He bought enough supplies to last about a week."

"Bugs was going to Castle Island. As soon as Harry gets his boat fixed we're going to the island. Maybe we can find a trail from there." Amy handed some of the pictures of Bugs to Paulo." Maybe you might give some of his pictures out, too. In the meantime I'm going to that hotel you mentioned. Your sister is a lovely young woman. Do you have a list of her friends?"

"Frankie didn't have any friends. She was very careful since she was here without papers. She went to the movies sometimes....alone. She didn't hang out in bars and she didn't date anyone. Her life was working to make money to send to our Mother. She was a really good girl."

"Where is the Blue Dolphin Hotel?"

"Take a right out the door. Keep the water on your left. It's about a mile from here."

"I can walk. It's good exercise."

"Amy, thank you so much for helping me. I love my sister."

Wandering around, she picked up a notebook and a Bic pen. When she was at the orphanage she was never without a writing pad in case she had an idea. "How much?"

"No charge to you."

"I'll find her, Paulo. I promise you."

She found Jimmy sound asleep topside. Harry came out of the cabin to talk to her.

"He told me that Bugs stopped at the store for supplies before he left."

"He's a nice guy. So since there's nothing more I can do right for now. I'm going to the Blue Dolphin Hotel to see what I can find out about his sister, Frankie. She used to work there. Do I have time before we're ready to go?"

"Sure. The parts came so I'm working on it. Take my car." He handed Amy the keys.

When she started to object he continued in a way that made sense. "The road to the Blue Dolphin is narrow. Not a good idea to be walking around."

"Thanks, Harry. I'll be extra careful."

"You better." Harry smiled. "Jimmy said if anything happened to you it would be very bad for him."

Amy laughed. "What?"

"When I got back without you he said he was a Leprechaun with magical powers, only taller than most, and that nothing better happen to you or Serena would turn him into a yard gnome." They both laughed. Only Amy knew it wasn't a joke. It was a fact that Jimmy's powers didn't work on or near water and from what she could see they were on the water and headed for an island in the middle of the Bermuda Triangle!

"I promise I will be back and Jimmy will not turn into anything!" As she walked away her thoughts turned to what Paulo said about Frankie not having any friends. She believed all young girls have at least one friend. She just had to find her.

Finding The Blue Dolphin Hotel was easy. There was a huge sign with blue dolphins leaping into the air over the turquoise waters of the ocean. It was more a two story motel than a hotel and it was in run down condition. There were ten units down and ten up with parking in front of the lower level rooms. Everything looked like it needed a coat of paint. The rusted black metal stairs leading to the second floor, on either end of the motel, were in desperate need of attention. The office was located right off the road. Attached to the office was a cafe. A neon sign proclaimed no vacancy but for those who were staying they offered free TV in the rooms and free breakfast in the Blue Dolphin Cafe. In the middle of the courtyard there was a chain link fence around an in-ground pool. A bunch of kids were in the pool while their parents sat in plastic chairs clustered around greasy, glass topped patio tables. Amy could understand why Frankie was eager to quit this place and get a better job. She sat in one of the chairs and waited until three housekeepers came out of a downstairs room throwing dirty laundry into a large wheeled hamper. A TV game show blared out of the open door. Before they had a chance to go back into the room Amy quickly walked up and started a conversation.

"Hello. I'm doing a freelance article for a Mexican Magazine about how tourists from Mexico like visiting Key West. Anyone here from Mexico?" Amy smiled and opened her notebook, pen poised.

One of the girls rudely flung her hand in the air and rattled off something in a language that sounded like she came from one of the Eastern European countries. The other girl agreed in the same language then they snatched up large bottles of a pink colored fluid, and cleaning rags from the supply cart, and went back inside the room they had been cleaning.

The third girl started collecting clean towels from a bottom shelf on the cart. "I from Mexico." She spoke in a whisper, making sure no one was listening. "You go room at end. Numero ten, no lock. I take break soon. I come."

Amy nodded okay and walked off. She casually strolled up to room ten and after looking around she opened the door and went inside. The room was cool and ready for the next guest. Dingy curtains were closed, letting in only a sliver of light. She sat on the edge of a vinyl armchair and waited. She didn't have to wait long. The door opened and the girl came inside.

"I Carmen. I only girl from Mexico."

"Carmen, I'm looking for Frankie. Did you know her? She used to work here. Do you know where she is?"

"She disappear. Frankie my friend. No say to anyone here about her."

"My name is Amy Lafitte. I'm a private detective. Her brother told me she had a job interview and then she disappeared. Here is a poster he gave me."

Carmen took the poster and smiled in a sad way when she saw Frankie's picture. "Frankie good girl. We go to movies sometime. Other girls from Romania here. They bad girls. I lonely now. You please find her." She handed Amy the poster. "Better I not have this. If other girls see, it bad for me."

"I understand. I promise you I will do everything I can to find her. You can help me. Can you tell me about the job offer? Frankie said she accepted an offer of a good job."

"Man and woman stay here. She say he a Reverend. They come many times and take girls go work in hotel on island. Mr. Greg, bad man, own this hotel, also from same place. He friend with Reverend. Frankie tell me man offer big cooking job. Frankie good cook."

"Which island, where?"

"No se. Frankie dice she send nota... sorry...letter, but I no hear nada."

"Carmen, this is important. Frankie left last November 18th. Can you check the hotel register and tell me the name of the man and the woman who offered Frankie that job. They stayed here at the time and they would have listed their address. Can you do this?"

"I try. You wait here." She left her basket of cleaning supplies on the floor. Amy saw an English to Romanian translation paperback next to a bottle of Windex.

Carmen was gone for what seemed like a long time. Amy heard a commotion going on upstairs. Suddenly Carmen was back with a paper in her hand. "I write down name. Go quick. I say something bad happen upstairs so Carlos leave desk rapido. When he go check I look in big book. I write down names."

Amy scanned the paper Carmen handed her. "Carmen, this is important...were the Reverend and his wife Romanian?"

Carmen looked at her in surprise. "Si. They speak same as other girls. Same as owner, Mr. Greg. That important?"

"Might be. I see you have an English to Romanian book so you can understand what the girls you work with are saying?"

"Yes, I find in bookstore."

"Perfect. I don't have time to buy one. Will you loan me yours?"

"Si." Carmen pulled out a dog eared paperback and handed it to Amy. "I do anything to help for Frankie."

"You've really helped. I promise you I will find Frankie."

Carmen gave Amy a hug. "You go quick now before they come. I go out first. If okay I knock on door." She pointed to the left. "Car park that way."

When Amy heard the knock she left, clutching the paper in her hand. She got back to her car and read what Carmen had copied from the hotel register. On November 18 a Reverend Damian and his wife, Madame Sonya, checked out. They had listed their address as

Castle Island. Amy was almost sure if she checked further she'd find the Reverend was somewhere around when there were other disappearances, too. Why Frankie and Bugs disappeared she had no idea but she was determined to find them. She was sure their disappearance was connected to Reverend Damian.

Amy parked Harry's car, in the same spot, next to the Marina store. She quickly briefed Paulo on what she had learned so far and asked him to keep any information she gave him private. "I promise I will find her."

When Amy got back to the boat she found Jimmy and Harry working on something in the cabin. Sitting on the deck she pulled out the book Carmen had loaned her and started reading. Being a fast reader she committed a lot of words and phrases to memory before Harry came looking for her.

"Did you find what you were looking for?" Harry noticed the book she was reading.

"Definitely. Did you get the engine fixed?"

"Definitely." She liked that Harry was funny and smart at the same time and he didn't ask her a million questions. She would tell him at her own pace and he instinctively knew that. Serena would approve. Of that she was sure.

The owner of the Blue Dolphin Hotel was sitting alone by the pool watching his grandson swim. A few minutes ago the pool had been crowded but at the sound of heavy thunder and serious flashes of lightning the guests had scattered for their rooms. He waved to Sylvie, one of the housekeepers. She hurried over at his side.

"Yes, Mr. Greg."

"I saw a young lady get in her car. She's not a guest, is she?"

"No, Mr. Greg." Of the Romanian housekeepers she spoke English the best. "She said she was writing an article for a magazine in Mexico. She wanted to know how people from Mexico liked visiting Key West."

"And what did you say?"

She thought fast. She hadn't talked to the woman. She had continued cleaning the apartment with Marla but she knew it would make Mr. Greg happy if she pretended that she said good things and mentioned his name, too. "I tell her they have a fantastic time if they come to Blue Dolphin because Mr. Greg, the owner, treats his guests like family."

"Very good, Sylvie. Very good."

He dismissed the girl but he had a nagging feeling this wasn't the end of it. That reporter, if she was a reporter, was going to be trouble.

CHAPTER FIVE

A Big Storm in the Middle of the Bermuda

Triangle

"Ready to go?"

"I am." Amy loved the sleek white sailboat.

"Here comes Paulo. Hey Jimmy..." Harry yelled down below. "Can you come up here and catch the lines? We're casting off."

Paulo passed two canvas bags full of snacks to Harry. "I am to give these to Miss Amy."

"Thanks for bringing them. What do I owe you?"

"Not a thing. You always put everything on account. You're one of my best customers. You pay your bill at the end of the month." Paulo smiled.

Jimmy caught the lines and neatly coiled them on deck.

Amy waved as Harry started up the engine. "Paulo, don't worry. We'll find Frankie." He felt her confidence. *"Nos vemos. That means see you later. Never goodbye."*

Amy wished she had something more positive to say.

Harry was busy maneuvering the boat away from the pier.

When they finally cleared the Marina he gave the engines full power. "Jimmy, you make a great first mate."

Amy could hear busy kitchen sounds from below. She really hoped it had something to do with Jimmy cleaning up the mess he was making. She sat down and watched the expert way Harry handled the boat. She imagined him as captain of his own pirate ship.

"I just hope we find this island before we run out of snacks." Amy raised her voice so Jimmy could hear her. "Then we'll just let him use his Leprechaun powers and materialize more bags of chips!"

Jimmy heard her. Surprisingly all crinkling of potato chip bags ceased. Laughing she let the wind carry her long hair behind her in a swirl of black silk. "It's so quiet. And peaceful."

"Enjoy it right now. We are headed into the Bermuda Triangle where just about anything can happen."

"I bet there are a lot of interesting things to see?"

"Lots of sunken pirate ships with chests of gold and jewels under the water we are crossing right now. How is that for exciting? And for the bird lovers there's Bird Island!"

"What is Bird Island?" Jimmy appeared from the main cabin below clutching a bag of Doritos. "Want anything?" When nobody was interested he continued munching.

Harry explained, "It's near the Bahamas. If we continued straight ahead we'd run into it. There are exotic birds on that island that can't be seen anywhere else in the world."

"I'd like to see Bird Island." Amy stopped Jimmy from disappearing below deck again by handing him the book she had been studying. "Look this over. By the way, I learned the Reverend and his wife are from Romania. They also have Romanian girls working for them at the Castle. It's like some kind of hotel where they put someone in touch with a loved one who died through séances and there's a Fortune Teller and some mystical magical events!

Jimmy grinned. "I bet they don't do that for free."

"I bet you're right. I talked to Paulo in the Marina store. His sister, Frankie, disappeared a few months ago. He told me she worked at the Blue Dolphin Hotel down the beach. I went there and talked to Carmen, a friend of Frankie. She told me Frankie was hired by the Reverend to work for his Hotel on Castle Island. And then she disappeared. I don't think it was coincidence that both Bugs and Frankie disappeared after having contact with the Reverend."

Jimmy knew exactly what she was saying. "I don't think it's a coincidence either. I bet it's a Hotel that offers phony tarot card readings, too." He thought about the tarot card readers in the French Quarter. Especially one lovely girl who was about his height too. He just found it hard to get involved and then have to tell them he was over two hundred years older than they were. He found it hard to lie and his love life suffered from that.

Amy nodded. "Memorize some words. Since they're a Romanian group it would be a good idea to know what they are saying to each other."

Jimmy took the book and carefully made his way to the front of the boat so he could sit, with his back against the main mast, and read.

Amy knew Harry was thinking about what Jimmy had said and worried about her safety. "Harry, the ones you have to worry about are the ones who don't advertise what they do." She turned and went below to the lounge.

It didn't make him feel better but he occupied his thoughts by reading a nautical map and charting a route to Castle Island.

Amy appeared on deck wearing an apron with a big green alligator on it and the message below it that read LOUISIANA YARD DOG. She laughed. "Where did you get this?"

"I picked it up at the New Orleans airport."

Amy handed him the apron.

"I think this is a hint. So are you guys ready for some sandwiches?"

"Oh yes, please!" Jimmy temporarily gave up his reading when he heard major food was coming up.

"How about my specialty...chicken egg salad?"

"I don't think I've ever had that but it sounds great."

"Good. Take the wheel. I'll make you the house special."

One more thing he liked about this girl...she was not a picky eater. He disappeared into the galley and came back a short time later with a picnic hamper.

Amy opened the hamper like it was a Christmas present. She was thrilled to find chicken egg salad sandwiches made with baked chicken, hard boiled eggs, parsley, celery and mayonnaise. "How did you do this? There was no time to cook a chicken."

"Paulo makes great Rotisserie chicken. And I picked up some hard boiled eggs, for the egg salad. You will also find some deli potato salad and chocolate chip cookies. Hey, Jimmy!"

The smell alone brought Jimmy out of the world of English to Romanian translations. "Whoa!" He laughed and set about digging into the hamper and coming out with paper plates for the sandwiches and cookies along with bowls and forks for the potato salad. "I'll get the drinks."

"Oh no! I forgot to get any." Harry just remembered it was the last thing on his list."

"Wait!" She came back with small bottles of frosty Martinelli's Apple Cider.

Harry sat back in the pilot's seat and had the best picnic he ever had.

"I never thought about adding Chicken to Egg Salad." Amy loved the combination.

"It was my Mom's recipe."

She knew when to ask questions and when to wait for someone to tell you on their own, at their own time. Gathering the empty plates, forks and juice bottles she disappeared below to tidy things up.

Jimmy went back to his book on English to Romanian which he was picking up rather quickly.

No one noticed that there was a storm behind them catching up at a fast pace.

Amy came back topside and peered around Harry at the clouds in the distance. "Uh, oh!"

Jimmy looked up from his book. Harry looked over his shoulder.

He saw big weather heading their way. The clouds were the darkest gray he'd ever seen. "Sometimes these storms come out of nowhere with huge waves, a lot of rain, big winds, bolts of lightning, rolling thunder and then they're gone."

"Oh, is that all? And...I didn't hear the other part of sometimes."

"Sometimes...they are really bad."

Amy raised her hand in the air to catch the breeze. She closed her eyes. "This one is not going to be too bad but we're going to be hit by a huge bolt of lightning and lose everything electrical."

Jimmy shoved the book he had been studying into a waterproof bag and closed it. "No rogue waves, no turning the boat over?"

"No, but get below. I don't want you to blow away. The winds are going to be fierce."

"Amy, hold the wheel. I'm going to secure down everything." Harry wondered how Amy was so sure about the weather. "Did you ever consider being a weather girl on TV?" He called over his shoulder.

He disappeared below deck and reappeared with a small black box, with a red switch, that he slipped into his pocket. Just as he finished tying down the mainsail the huge storm descended upon them with rain, thunder, lightning, strong winds and very large waves. In the past he had been in big storms, in the air and on his boat, so knew the routine. He did everything by the book. What he didn't plan on was the lightning bolt that hit the deck, curled around and went right for the engine below the floor boards. Immediately everything electrical went out. He could smell the frying wires. It was a battle to keep the boat from going sideways against the huge waves.

Jimmy watched as his precious snacks were floating in water that covered the floor. He just wished he could pull out his gold dust and make everything right but he had no power over or around water. What a mess!

Amy knew that the boat would make it but it was still scary. She marveled at how expertly Harry handled the wheel.

The storm disappeared as fast as it had arrived. They were left with calm waters and blue skies. The bad part was there was no wind and worse, no engine.

Harry yelled down below, "Jimmy are you okay?"

"I'm fine but the food is floating in about a foot of water."

Amy smiled. "Good thing we had something to eat."

"Good thing." Harry thought any other female would be wailing right now but Amy looked cool and collected. Great woman to have by his side in an emergency. "Jimmy, hand me the binoculars."

"Where are they?"

"In the cabinet behind the sofa."

They heard a lot of splashing then Jimmy appeared on deck with the binoculars. He stood up on a bench seat and scanned the horizon. Excited he ran towards the bow with the binoculars. "Harry, there's an island out there with a big house, looks like a castle. It must be Castle Island!" Jimmy was shouting and jumping up and down with joy.

"That's where we're going. Let me see."

Amy passed Harry the binoculars. She could feel the tug of waves as they were being pulled away from land. "Oh, great. No wind, no sails. We can't exactly row there and we're being pulled out to sea by the current."

Harry thought about his Sat phone and remembered he had left it below earlier, when he was working on the engine. He asked Jimmy to check anyway. Jimmy came back with a melted phone.

"It's not working." Jimmy shook his head and passed it over.

Harry was out of options. He pulled the black box out of his pocket and flipped the red switch on. The emergency beacon went right to the office at Morgan Air. When his Dad was gone, like right now, Joey took over as office manager but he happened to be out of the office at the moment so the flashing red light, on top of the file cabinet, went unnoticed.

Pulling the Romanian language book from his back pocket Jimmy returned to sitting with his back against the main mast, concentrating as best he could. He looked out at the calm water just in time to see grey fins headed right for their disabled boat. It looked like millions of them. Jimmy jumped up and started screaming...."Sharks!! Sharks!! We're like a shark buffet! Help! Someone help!" He dropped his book and ran back and forth on the bow. He ran to the railing to get a better view and not watching his footing, he went right over the side of the boat. He went down like a concrete statue, right into the path of the grey fins.

Harry didn't hesitate, he dove head first into the still rippling waters, swimming towards the last place he'd seen Jimmy go down. He saw Jimmy about ten feet down, gyrating in crazy moves, with his hands and feet going in different directions. Harry grabbed him from behind and hauled him up to the surface.

"Amy, take him!" He pushed Jimmy up in the air, one foot on the stairs for support.

Amy hauled him up and sat him down on the deck. "Jimmy, breathe, it's okay, you can breathe now."

Harry joined them on deck. "I didn't see any sharks. Do you mean the Dolphins?"

"Right there!" Jimmy pointed in the direction of four, huge Dolphins who suddenly leaped out of the water.

Amy heard them silently saying, *We're Dolphin Rescue at your service!*

Jimmy continued. "I swear I saw sharks. I saw their fins. I bet the Dolphins scared them away."

"Seriously, Jimmy. Dolphins have fins, too. But these guys came when I called for help. By the way they are called Dolphin Rescue.*"*

Amy silently spoke to them, *I'm Amy. The one jumping up and down is Jimmy and the one behind me is Harry.*

Hi there, Amy. I'm Melody. The big one is called Grande. The other two shy boys are Harp and Flute. We used to be part of the Water Dance Show at Dolphin World in Miami until the last hurricane shut us down. After that we took to the open sea. Would you please tell Jimmy we are not sharks. Geez, there's a big difference!

Grande whistled. *Yeah, big difference. We don't eat the people we help!*

Jimmy's face turned beet red.

Amy smiled and jabbed him in the side. "Scared of big old Dolphins?"

"You said you called for help. What do you have a Dolphin Help Line?" Harry was watching the acrobatic show the four oversized Dolphins were putting on.

"I guess this is something I'm going to have to explain." Amy sighed.

"You definitely guessed right."

"Especially since I'm now going to ask you to throw four lines off the bow so they can tow us to the island."

"Oh man, good thing I'm never going to tell anyone about this. No one would believe me anyway."

"Serena would."

"Serena talks to Dolphins, too?" Harry was amazed once again.

Jimmy jumped into the conversation. "Amy and Serena talk to most animals...the smart ones."

"Well let's give these smart Dolphins something to do. They need four tow lines."

"Coming up." Harry lifted one of the side benches and took out four tow lines.

"I see you've been towed before." Amy couldn't contain a laugh.

"Yeah, but not by Dolphins!" He quickly secured two lines to the bow and one to each side.

Melody leaped out of the water close to Jimmy and gave him a wink before she snatched the line up in her surprisingly strong jaws. The other Dolphins grabbed a line and went to work. The hard part was getting the boat moving, after that it was easy. Easy, that is, until the wind suddenly started up, blowing against them. Two feet ahead, three feet back. This time the Dolphins called for help.

While they were being towed Harry asked Amy. "Can you read minds? Like what I'm thinking?"

"Yes." Amy blushed.

"We both can. That's kindergarten stuff." Jimmy answered.

Harry recalled thinking how incredible Amy was and how much he liked her and all the time she knew exactly what he was thinking. He smiled. "Can you teach me to do that?"

"Maybe." Amy put that on her list to ask Serena.

"Any other talents you want to tell me about?"

"Serena gave me the power to touch something and, if I ask, I can go back in time and see where that object has been."

"I bet that comes in handy with detective work." "It does."

The tow was slow going. Soon they had three more Dolphins pushing from the stern.

"They said they worked with Melody in Miami. We are not their first rescue but I'm the only human, so far, that can hear them. They said they are really happy to help us." Amy could just imagine how that sounded but sooner or later she would have to tell Harry many things that were a lot stranger.

Joey saw the red light blinking on top of the file cabinet the minute he returned. He knew Harry wouldn't hit that button unless he was in trouble. Calling the hanger he ordered a jet helicopter to stand by. Once airborne he called Paulo and told him the situation. Paulo said he would have a fast boat ready for him the minute he touched down at the Marina.

The minute the helicopter landed Paulo raced out and pointed to a very powerful speed boat that was ready to go. Tow lines were coiled in the well of the boat. Just in case he took the emergency food pack Paulo handed him that held water and sandwiches. "Thanks, Paulo." Firing up the engines he took off, careful of the speed limit inside the Marina. When he cleared the breakwater, and was into open water, he fired up the two powerful engines. Joey followed the GPS to the other black box secure in Harry pocket.

The Dolphin tow approached the island. When the fog shifted Amy could see a huge gothic castle very close to the shoreline. A dense forest surrounded it. The dark grey stone exterior of the castle looked cold and uninviting. The entire island was shrouded in a heavy fog that was moving very slowly. Harry had never seen anything so ominous. The whole place looked haunted.

"It might be." Amy answered.

Harry was still not used to her reading his thoughts.
She smiled.

Before he had time to reply they were at the landing and Jimmy had tossed the lines to the dock before jumping over and securing the boat fore and aft to wood pilings.

Amy was sure they came in so quietly no one knew they were there. At that moment she heard movement outside the house. Guessing there were hidden cameras, and someone had finally noticed Castle Island had guests, she waited and wondered about the welcome they would be getting.

Amy turned to the Dolphins. *Thanks for the tow. You all were great!*

Anytime. Just give us a shout out! The Dolphins disappeared.

Harry decided to be silent. He would let Amy do the talking.

She gracefully jumped onto the dock.

A tall thin man with black hair and wearing black ceremonial robes that swept the ground when he walked, strolled down the crooked pier followed by a woman wearing a similar robe. They were trailed by a procession of men and women dressed very casually.

Amy immediately spotted two in the procession that she recognized. Marsha and Mark had been Murder Mystery Dinner Party guests at the Devereux Plantation. Before Marsha could say a word Amy nodded her head to the group behind the Reverend and greeted them. "Hello. I'm Amy, this is my friend, Jimmy, and our guide, Harry."

"Greetings and welcome. I am Reverend Damian, this is my wife, Madame Sonya and these are our guests. You have landed at Ravensclaw, a Bed & Breakfast for spiritual healing."

"We didn't so much as land here," Amy explained, "It was more like our boat had an electrical problem, just as we were passing, and luckily we were pushed here by the waves."

"Passing? Where were you going? We are in the middle of nowhere."

The answer came to Amy in an instant. Thank goodness it was something Harry had said..."Bird Island. We were on our way to visit Bird Island. "

The Reverend had a pensive look on his face. "I've heard of it but I don't think I have ever been there. I'm not overly fond of birds as so many are. We have many Ravens on our little island."

Amy wondered about someone who called fifty private acres a 'little island.'"

Suddenly a powerful boat engine filled the air space with fumes and noise.

Amy raised her voice to be heard. "I do believe a rescue tow is here for our Bird Island guide."

Harry waved and hopped on the rescue craft that had pulled alongside his boat.

Before he could say a word Amy gave him a severe look and yelled out, "I am not taking my life in my hands and riding in that disabled craft. I suggest you go take care of your repairs and call me. We can then proceed to that Bird place."

"Sorry." He called back. He admired the way she handled the situation.

"Jimmy, do you have my mobile?" "Uh, nope."

"My dear lady, it would do you no good anyway." The Reverend was watching Amy carefully, still not sure about these two who appeared out of nowhere. "There is no cell phone service from the island but we do have a land line."

Amy turned and said. "Well I don't have my mobile anyway. I'm sure my guide can reach me at your lovely mansion."

The entire group stood there fascinated by the rescue maneuvers. Harry threw out towlines from the rescue boat and then secured them between the two boats. Meanwhile Jimmy cast the lines from the dock back to Harry's boat, "Gone fishing." Harry took the wheel and with a snap of the lines the rescue boat started the tow with a spray of sea water.

With a final dismissive look in the direction of her Bird Island guide Amy turned to Reverend Damian and said, "This has been such an ordeal. I hope you will take mercy on me and my friend, Jimmy." She dramatically waved her hands. "I can sense the fabulous history of Ravensclaw. Do you have rooms for a brief stay? I can definitely pay. I just inherited a large sum of money and an estate." Amy detected a gleam in the Reverend's eyes when she mentioned the inheritance.

"Of course. We always have room for our friends in distress." He patted her arm. "My wife Madame Sonya is a world famous fortune teller. She's from Egypt, you know! You would do well to consult her on your future travels."

"I will. Thank you." Amy looked up with a shy smile on her face. She might be only nineteen but she was wise enough to the ways of the world.

"Well, enough chat for now. We must make haste inside to a warm fire and a lovely tea."

She studied the Reverend and his wife as they took the lead. Both were way past middle age. The Reverend dyed his thinning hair, moustache and goatee black. He looked more French than Romanian. His face bore lines of a life spent conning and lying. His expanding girth was not quite hidden by his long robe. His wife looked like a little doll with blond curls and big blue eyes. When you looked closer you could see there was more silver than blonde in her hair. Lines below her eyes and around her mouth told a story about her age.

"Amy, you didn't tell us where you and your friend are from." The Reverend had dropped back to walk next to her.

"I was born in London and spent most of my life on a private island off Scotland. Jimmy is from Ireland." Amy reverted to the English accent she had learned from living at the orphanage. "Of course we have traveled quite a bit..."

"I've never been to the UK. You must tell me all about it. Our guests, Lady Catherine and her ladies maid, Miranda, are from Great Britain. I'm sure you will have lots to talk about." The Reverend came to a stop. With a wave of his hand a young girl appeared and took Amy's small valise and Jimmy's backpack, which he struggled to hold onto. "Jimmy, please let Marta take your luggage inside. Come along now before we all catch a death of a cold. This storm has turned the winds a bit cold, don't you think?" The Reverend took Amy's arm and linked it through his. She thought his fingers felt like cold fish fins.

"I can't agree more." As Amy passed Marsha she nodded her head and said, "Hello, lovely place, isn't it?" She was grateful to have an excuse to get away from the Reverend who walked on by dropping back to talk to Lady Catherine, a fellow Brit. Amy noticed Lady Catherine and Miranda didn't say a word. Lady Catherine just nodded her head.

Marsha knew exactly who they were and understood Amy and Jimmy were traveling incognito as they were, too. "My husband, Mark, and I have often talked about going to London. We'll have to have a chat sometime."

Amy joined her as they walked. "I would love that."

Jimmy, I sure don't trust that Reverend and his fake Egyptian Fortune Teller wife.

Be careful!

Why? The Reverend can't hear us!

A new voice joined the conversation. *I can! My name is Margaret. You're right though so don't worry, no one else can. My husband, Ray and I are from New Orleans. I heard you talking to the Dolphins. Did they really give you a tow to the island?*

They did indeed. What's with the Reverend? He looks like a con artist.

You're very perceptive. I don't trust him either. Be careful what you say out loud. The whole island is wired with cameras and listening devices. When you formally meet us the Reverend will say we're from New Orleans. You comment that you're looking forward to visiting New Orleans. I'll say I would be happy to show you around the French Quarter. Then I'll offer to show you around the island. I have a lot to tell you.

Thank you, Margaret.

Amy rejoined the fast paced Reverend but staying on the uneven stone pathway, kept conversation to a minimum.

The fog was so thick it was hard to see the details of the gothic castle. Finally they were in front of massive entrance doors in the middle of a round Tower made of cold dark grey stone with multi-paned windows. Smoke poured from one of the numerous chimneys that reached into the sky above the roofline.

The Reverend held a massive door open and everyone entered a large, circular stone room. An open fire, against a back wall, welcomed them. To the right was an open door that revealed steep, winding stairs that presumably led to the top of the tower.

A young girl, wearing a knee length navy blue dress with a white lace collar stood ready to accept coats and hats from the guests.

"Marta, please tell Sylvie to add more chairs to the group. Our new guests will be staying in the East Wing. Take their things there. At once!"

Amy was aware of the sound of dripping water, coming from her valise and Jimmy's backpack, onto the slate floor.

"Oh, no!"

"Never you mind. My staff will take care of your things. Everything will be cleaned, dried and returned to your rooms after dinner."

Marta rushed out with their things.

Unburdened of their coats and hats the guests followed the Reverend through an open gothic arch into a great room on the left. Amy and Jimmy were the last to enter.

The Reverend sat in a wing chair flanked, in a semi-circle, by overstuffed chairs. The guests took their seats like they were in class taking their assigned seats. Amy and Jimmy took the only two vacant seats at the end.

Two young girls, wearing the same navy blue uniforms, were pouring and serving tea. Trays of tiny sandwiches and sweet cakes were heaped on silver trays atop two mahogany sideboards against the wall. Jewel toned Persian rugs covered the wood floors. A huge fire in a massive stone fireplace made the cavernous room warm and cozy.

Reverend Damian leaned forward to talk to Amy and Jimmy. "In two days we plan on taking our guests to a festival in Key West." He smiled. "I'd like you to meet the group. Margaret and Ray are from New Orleans. Marsha and Mark are from Northern California. Lady Catherine is here with her ladies maid, Miranda.

They are from England." Lady Catherine gave me a royal wave. "Dr. Lowery and Delta are from North Carolina. Their husbands are off for a day of fishing."

"Where in North Carolina?" Amy knew all about the beautiful state of North Carolina. Blackbeard, who was from North Carolina, had married a Claiborne a few centuries ago. And Amy was a Claiborne on her Mother's side.

Dr. Lowery spoke first, "I have a Dental practice in Cary, North Carolina. Close to Durham and Raleigh."

"The pirate, Blackbeard, is from North Carolina. I'd love to talk later."

She caught Margaret's eye, "Reverend Damian said you're from New Orleans! It's the next place on our list to visit. It's supposed to be a fantastic city. Any recommendations?"

"Oh yes, there are tons of great places to eat, wonderful plantations to visit and nowhere is more enchanting then the French Quarter. In fact, the small hotels in the French Quarter are more charming then the big five star hotels. If you like I'd be happy to show you around the island tomorrow and I can tell you what to see and do in New Orleans."

"That would be wonderful."

"Let's go after breakfast. It's such a large island." Margaret smiled and took a sip of her tea.

The Reverend sighed loudly, rudely interrupting any further communication. Amy could tell he hated not being the center of attention. "If you're not too tired perhaps you, and your friend Jimmy, will join us after dinner for the séance."

Amy quickly spoke up. "I wouldn't miss it! I've never been to a séance before."

Jimmy smiled and agreed. It was all a show. He really thought séances were phony baloney meant to part someone from their jewels, money or both.

Amy sent a silent message. *Jimmy, the Reverend is taking everyone to Key West in a few days?*

I heard. Don't worry so much!

Margaret interrupted to add, "Reverend Damian, we really don't travel much but I read online that Ravensclaw is a haunted castle and in the past you held Murder Mystery Dinner Parties. They are said to be quite famous."

"How wonderful! I've always wanted to go to one of those." Amy turned to the Reverend. "Are you having the Murder Mystery anytime soon? We could extend our stay, in that case. I hope we are still in time."

The Reverend stood and with a dramatic flair turned and faced his guests. "With the new Pirate Fest starting soon I decided to hold the Murder Mystery Dinner Party tomorrow night. I haven't had time to tell everyone about the change in plans but I know all of you will be thrilled. Turning to Amy he said, "And for our new guests, you are welcome to participate in everything and stay as long as you want."

Amy clapped her hands. "I am thrilled! I don't know exactly what it is but it sounds brilliant."

Marsha used the chance to jump right in and give a reason why they were there, too. "Actually we didn't mention this before but we read the same online information and I said to Mark, we absolutely have to go! I've always wanted to attend a Murder Mystery Dinner Party. Maybe he will have one during our stay at Ravensclaw, and see I was right!"

Reverend Damian smiled at his guests. "All our plans were set for next week but because of Pirate Fest in Key West we will have all our activities this week instead. So it's settled. The séance tonight and the Murder Mystery Dinner Party tomorrow night. We leave for Key West on Friday. We'll stay at the fabulous Blue Dolphin Hotel. They have their own private beach and, of course, everything is paid for. Pirate Fest starts the day we arrive so we will leave Ravensclaw early, get settled, and take in all the festivities."

Amy looked at the Reverend. "And to think all this fun came from information online. Looks like advertising does pay."

"Yes, it does, doesn't it?" The Reverend sat down.

Jimmy, The Blue Dolphin Hotel! That's where I went looking for information on Frankie. You have no idea what a dump his fabulous Blue Dolphin Hotel really is. It's awful. It looked like a rundown motel with a dirty pool, cheap bedspreads and a trash filled beach.

Jimmy had to look down to keep from laughing out loud. *Oh wow! You make it sound so appealing.*

Believe me, that was the good part! Listen, I would just bet this is their last con job. I think when they drop everyone at that cheap hotel they are going to make a mad dash out of the country, probably with the two million cash and all the gold and jewels they've stolen from guests over the years.

I bet you're right.

They soon finished their tea and biscuits.

Amy yawned. This had been a very exciting day. "I think I'll go lay down before dinner."

The Reverend approved. "Very good idea. Dinner is at seven but we don't stand on formality. Oh, by the way, I asked staff to put Mumu's in your rooms if you'd like to wear them to dinner. They are much like the ones my dear wife and I wear. I imagine your clothes must be a bit wet. We will take care of your things."

"Thank you! That is very kind."

Jimmy and Amy followed the maid, Marta, up the wide mahogany staircase. Marta stopped in front of a door at the end of a long corridor on the second floor. "Miss Amy you are in the Rose Suite and Mr. Jimmy you are right across the hall in the Blue Room." She handed them their keys. "Your dinner attire is in your room. The Reverend asked that we unpack for you. We already took away your wet things to be cleaned and dried." Marta disappeared down the hall.

Jimmy followed Amy into her room grumbling non-stop. "Why do you get a suite and I get a room?"

Amy sat down on the very comfortable four poster bed and whispered. "Because, my dear friend, I am an heiress and deserve any and all comforts in life." *Jimmy, watch what you say. I'm sure everything is being recorded. Tomorrow when I say I'm going for a walk with Margaret you demand to go, too. We can talk then. Until tomorrow...not a word because I'm sure everything is being recorded.*

I want to search this place. I believe Bugs was taken prisoner and he's nearby."

Me, too, but we have a lot of places to look and it's a big island. "I'm still miffed that you got the bigger room!"

Amy spied a lovely dress placed over a chair in the room. It was a hooded navy blue silk velvet, floor length gown. Amy loved the side pockets. A good place to put your room key.

In the meantime act and talk normally. "Look at this lovely gown they loaned me. I think I'll wear it to dinner." Amy ushered Jimmy out the door. "I need my beauty sleep so see you later."

"OK. I'll be right here at seven." Jimmy left wondering if his room was all in blue. If it was it would match his spirits. Today is Tuesday, tomorrow night is the Murder Mystery and everyone leaves for Key West the next day, on Thursday. They didn't have much time to figure it out.

Amy took a shower and washed her hair. After a short nap she put on the lovely dark blue silk velvet gown. She would have loved wearing the little black dress she had brought. After all an heiress, even a fake one, could dress exactly as she wanted to as long as it wasn't being cleaned!

Jimmy started banging on her door. Where was she? She was late. Dinner started a few minutes ago. The last thing he wanted to do was irritate their host if they wanted to get information from him.

Amy finally opened her door. *You are still in your wet smelly things.* "She sniffed close to him. *"Excuse me...now damp smelly things. Why aren't you wearing the robe they gave you? You did get one?*

Yes, I did! And it made me look like a character actor in a TV movie called "Strange Planet?"

Any had a big smile as she waltzed right by Jimmy. He had to walk fast to keep up with her.

"Well, are you happy now, heiress Amy? We are going to be late for dinner. I like seeing your hair down for once."

"You think more of your stomach than anything else. Reverend Damian did say about seven'ish. We won't be the only ones late. Watch!"

CHAPTER SIX

Dinner and A Séance

She was wrong. Everyone was seated and waiting for them. The Reverend was on one end, his wife on the other. He stood and pulled out the chair on his left. "Miss Amy, over here."

Jimmy sat in the other empty seat at the end next to Miranda, Lady Catherine's maid. He had as little to say to her as she did to him which suited him just fine.

The dinner was excellent.

Amy watched Jimmy eat with such enthusiasm she was worried he would ask for seconds. The last thing she wanted to do was call attention to themselves.

"Any mushy peas left?" Jimmy asked with an innocent expression on his face.

Amy narrowed her eyes at him and forced her voice to drip honey. Even from one end of the table to the other Amy made her voice heard. "Jimmy, you must not eat our host out of house and home."

The distance between them made Jimmy defiant. He lifted his chin and spoke very clearly. "I was only asking for mushy peas, for Heaven's sake."

Amy was talking to the Reverend so Margaret turned to Jimmy. "Jimmy, what are mushy peas?"

"It's English." He turned his attention to Reverend Damian who was dying to make sure everyone knew he took excellent care of his guests.

"Oh, well, sure, why not." Margaret laughed.

"Dear boy," the Reverend jumped right in, "Of course we have more. Whatever you need don't hesitate to ask any of the staff. They are here to serve you." He waved his hand and a dining room server quickly left the room to alert the cook.

Amy spoke up trying to get the attention off of Jimmy who looked like he was about to explode. What was his problem? "So sorry, Reverend Damian. One would think we had been floating around on that boat for ages."

Reverend Damian looked up. "I thought no such thing. In fact didn't you say you were close to our little island when your boat lost power?"

Amy recovered quickly. "Why yes. And we were lucky we were since everything electrical was fried. The lightning, you know. Didn't you see the storm?"

"I'm afraid not. It was our meditating hour. We hold them every so often. The blackout drapes were drawn. And we were in a room facing the forest, not the water. But one of our staff finally saw you and alerted me."

"Thank you again for your wonderful hospitality. And I want to tell you that the Chef did a magnificent job with dinner." Amy just bet one of the staff saw them on the camera monitors. She could only think it was a miracle they didn't see the Dolphin Recue tow crew. How would she have explained that?

"She is good, isn't she? I have to tell the truth our chef is my wife, Madame Sonya."

"Please give her my compliments."

"I shall."

"I can't wait to attend the séance tonight. I hope I am invited."

"Of course you and your friend are invited! We sit on pillows in a circle. The more attendees, the stronger our link to the spiritual world. I am very glad you will join us."

"You have been very gracious to two travelers stranded at sea."

Amy, me dear, any second now I'm going to choke on your graciousness! What a lot of hooey!

Jimmy, please don't go to the séance if you plan on making a scene.

There is absolutely nothing else to do and I refuse to go to my hovel early! I plan on out graciousnessing you! Is that a word?

Amy narrowed her eyes at him. *Mind your manners. We are here to find Bugs and hopefully Frankie, too. Keep that in mind.*

Jimmy grumbled in response.

The Reverend stood and dropped his napkin on the table. Waving his hands in the air to get everyone's attention he gushed, "Everyone! Everyone! We will be meeting in the library at nine sharp. And our new friends, Amy and Jimmy, will be joining us for the séance. See you all there."

Amy checked her watch. They had fifteen minutes to find the library.

Marsha walked up and touched her arm. "I'll show you the way. My husband is not joining us. He takes a nightly walk after dinner."

"Jimmy, why don't you join Marsha's husband. It would be good for your constitution."

"And pass up the séance...good grief...NO!"

"Then let's go!"

Dr. Lowery's husband and Delta's husband, were also not going. They were exhausted from their day of fishing so they elected to stay in their room and read. When Margaret's husband, Ray, bowed out Jimmy and the Reverend became the only men in the company of the women. That was all right with him, he thought. He was there to protect Amy. If anything happened to her he was totally sure Serena, would make him into a bookend and that was the kindest thought he had about what his fate would be in her hands.

The library was an enormous room down the hall to the right. There was a fire blazing in a fireplace that was big enough for a man to walk into and sit down. The only light in the room was from the open fire and lit candles placed on tables around the room. Books were stacked on every shelf of carved rosewood bookcases that filled the walls.

In some spaces, where there would have been books, there were sculptures of ballerinas that were strikingly beautiful. Amy recognized an oil painting signed by Degas. She knew by reading Art

History books that Degas had lived on Esplanade in the French Quarter and was a famous painter of young ballerinas.

Jewel toned hand woven carpets covered the wood floors. It was the first time a library had been converted into the inside of a nomadic sheik's tent. Silk pillows, in vivid colors were placed in a circle. The ceiling was draped in a silk fabric with gold and silver threads running through each panel. The lit candles caught the precious metals and made the ceiling glitter.

One of the staff wheeled in a tea cart, groaning under the weight of silver trays, with a huge tea pot and pitchers of cream and sugar. Besides the tea cups, there were small glasses filled with thick Turkish coffee. Most tempting were the plates of delicate little petit fours and various cookies.

Amy expected to see Laurence of Arabia gallop by outside the massive floor to ceiling windows that looked out at the forest. This must be the Meditation Room, she thought.

Madame Sonya was seated on a high pillow that put her above the rest of the participants. Amy was amazed to see she had removed the scarf that had hidden her hair. Long and silver in color her hair flowed over her shoulders and down her back. She had changed from the robe she had been wearing on the dock into black velvet pants and a matching hooded tunic.

Waving her hand she invited Amy to sit on her right and Lady Catherine on her left. Everyone else followed, in no specific order, finding a pillow to sit on.

The Reverend sat opposite her with Jimmy beside him. Amy knew Jimmy hated to be touched so every time her friend squirmed out of the reach of the Reverend's cold fingers only made the determined man try to pinch his arm to get his attention. Poor Jimmy, Amy thought, he was doing his best not to make a scene. His face became almost as red as his hair!

Amy quickly looked back at the Madame before she started laughing.

Large ornate silver candelabras, on heavy trays to catch any wax that might fall, were placed in the middle of the circle. Everything was arranged to calm the spirits inside and out.

When the Reverend clapped his hands the staff lit the silver candelabras and left the library, quietly shutting the door.

For the first time Amy heard Madame Sonya speak. She had a deep voice with a pronounced Eastern European accent in broken English.

"Once I summon spirit guide no break contact with hands. If you leave seat spirit guide will punish you. Do all understand what I say? You know what you do? Yes?" Her intense gaze swept around the room, lingering briefly on each guest.

Everyone nodded.

"Then I begin."

Amy started to count the heavy gold bangles on Madame Sonya's wrist but her attention was taken by an ornate carved wooden box the woman retrieved from a large velvet drawstring bag that also held a pack of tarot cards. "Perhaps my spirit guide will be kind to us tonight and Lady Catherine's beloved daughter will appear to her distraught Mother."

Amy couldn't take her eyes off the ornate box that was placed so tantalizingly close to her. Chief Barker told her Bugs purchased a similar box prior to sailing to Ravensclaw. The owner of an antique store had seen a missing person flyer circulated around town and, recognizing Bugs, called the Police Chief. She had to find a way to touch the box. Serena had given her the power of touch. One touch and she could go back in time and see where the box had been.

"I ready now!" Madame Sonya and the Reverend reached out and everyone joined hands to close the circle. "I never know who spirit guide will be. I hope tonight my darling daughter, Triss. Please she come to me. She pass over many years ago."

Amy had to give the Madame a hand. By telling the guests she also had a darling daughter who had died she manipulated them into feeling connected to her. Thinking about touching the box was distracting. She had to pay attention to what Madame Sonya was doing.

The Madame threw her head back while moaning and calling out a name..."Triss, Triss, darling, please you help. Come! Triss, Triss?" She bent forward with her forehead almost touching the table and stayed that way for what seemed to Amy like a very long time. Finally lifting her head she sighed.

A sweet young voice floated through the air. "Yes, Mother, I'm here."

"My Darling. Long time you no visit. I miss terribly." The Madame's eyes filled with tears that coursed down her cheeks.

Amy had to hold back a smile. *Jimmy, now that's a Drama Queen!*

OH, so true, me dear! Now listen, If the table lifts or starts shaking, make a scene. I'll peek under and see if there are any mechanical devices.

What? You don't believe in the Madame? How shocking!

Amy, stop that! You are going to make me laugh. This is too hilarious for words.

159

Madame Sonya was crying and talking at once. "Remember I ask you find Lady Catherine's Camilla."

"I did, Mother."

"Lady Catherine want to hear Camilla voice. She love her. She say she miss her little Camilla terribly."

The voice sounded sad. "Cam Cam, says she suffers. She asks why she died. She wants to know if she can return."

Lady Catherine couldn't hold back her excitement. "That was my nickname for her...Cam Cam!"

Madame Sonya was angry. "Lady Catherine, no speak when I with spirit guide."

Lady Catherine bent her head.

The Madame continued. "Please ask Camilla appear this time. Lady Catherine need see her, just once. Please tell."

There was a long pause before the voice spoke again. "Camilla says she's not ready. Maybe later. She asks if Mother takes care of Mirabell?"

Madame Sonya spoke directly to Lady Catherine. "Okay, speak now."

Amy was amazed at the control Sonya was having over the conversation. She had to give it to her, she was definitely good at this phony séance stuff.

Lady Catherine, not able to hold back her anguish cried out, "Yes, my little Cam Cam, I love your little sweet, Mirabell. She sleeps in your bed. I take excellent care of her and every night I explain you send your love even if you are not with her. Do you remember the horrible accident that took you from us? If you appear to me it's like you are still here. Please come. I miss you and think of you every day."

Madame Sonya smiled. "Spirit guide say Camilla is pleased. She say maybe soon she appear."

There was a pause and then the voice of the spirit guide was speaking like it was very far away. "We have to go."

Lady Catherine cried out. "Don't leave, Darling. We had so little time together."

Madame Sonya looked around and realized everyone was expecting an explanation for why Camilla had not spoken to Lady Catherine. She let out a dramatic sigh. "I think big storm not good for celestial travel. Maybe next time."

Everyone stayed in their seats, not sure what to do next.

Madame Sonya held a hand to her forehead. "Please leave now. Perhaps you visit Madame Bettina, third floor. She read fortune. All go now. Reverend and I see you in morning. He tell me surprise breakfast at eight, very early, yes?" The Reverend led the group out of the room talking about what they planned for breakfast in the morning.

Everyone was talking about breakfast except Lady Catherine. She was still crying softly as she followed behind the guests. Amy heard her tell her ladies maid, Miranda, "Just once I want to hear her voice again. Just once." Their conversation was cut off when Madame Sonya shut the door behind her.

Amy and Jimmy were still sitting at the table when Madame Sonya returned. With a dramatic flourish she put the back of her hand to her head. "I have big pain in head. Contact spirit guide no easy. You go, please. I feel faint."

Amy wasn't fooled for one second. This woman was a barracuda. Passing out wasn't in her vocabulary.

"I wonder if I might look at that box." Amy indicated the ornately carved box that held the tarot cards. "There is writing on it. It's Ancient Aramaic. If I look at it I'll tell you what it says." She wasn't sure what it was but she could bet Madame didn't either.

Madame Sonya looked surprised and quickly sat down, ready to hear more. Her headache appeared to have magically disappeared. "You know such writing? Please tell me!" She pushed the box over to Amy who picked it up looking like she was studying it.

A bolt of lightning flashed outside the library window. Amy's hands tingled. Silently she asked to see the past. She felt like she was flying. She was enveloped in fog. The fog suddenly lifted and she was in a shop with wonderful antiques. She recognized Bugs Robichaux at once. He was buying an ornately carved box, exactly like the one she was holding. The dealer was showing him how to press the sharp ends of the crossed swords on a bottom of the box. A secret compartment, running the length of the box opened. After carefully putting the box in his small rolling luggage Bugs walked outside. Amy saw Bugs board a boat tied up at the dock. He cast off. Once out of sight of the mainland he placed the tightly rolled treasure map in the secret place in the box. Amy was at once surrounded by a heavy fog. The next thing Amy saw was Bugs in his bedroom. He was in a hurry, rushing around, packing. He made a quick decision and stood the antique box on end between three heavy books on the rosewood bookcase on the wall across from his bed. He picked up his bag and left the room. As he left Amy noted he was in Room 306.

"What does it say? What does it say?" Madame Sonya touched her arm and broke Amy's concentration.

She quickly made up something. "The writing is a warning. It says something about how this box must be placed where it was found and then the secret writing will tell the tale. I don't know what that means." Amy smiled sweetly.

"I do. Yes, I do. I will obey!" Madame Sonya snatched the box out of Amy's hands.

Amy almost laughed out loud. Sonya was a giant fake. She bet Jimmy was thinking the same thing. Right now she had to get her hands on the box long enough to remove the treasure map before the woman found the map herself. She started coughing violently hoping that would buy her time and opportunity.

Jimmy, I have to get my hands on that box again. Tell her I'm having a serious allergy attack and the only thing that will stop it is if I drink salt and water. I don't see any around so she will have to leave the table to get help.

Jimmy played his part very well. "Oh, my goodness!" Jimmy rushed around the table to comfort Amy. "Madame Sonya, Amy is having a severe allergic reaction to something in the room. I've seen it before. Please do you have salt and water? That is the only thing that will save her. She might choke to death!" Jimmy cried out in terror at the thought. "Oh, my dear friend, please do not die!" Jimmy ran around in a circle, wringing his hands.

Amy did all she could to keep from laughing, while pretending like she was choking, at the same time.

Dropping the box to the table Madame Sonya frantically pushed at something under the table. Nothing happened. She yelled for Marta. No one came to her aid.

Amy was beginning to wonder just how long she was going to have to continue coughing. She grabbed her throat, gasping for breath. Madame Sonya screamed in frustration and rushed to the library door to call for help.

The second the woman was out of sight Amy picked up the box, turned it over and quickly pressed the tips of the swords exactly like the antique shop owner had done. A drawer slid open. She removed the treasure map and pushed it into the deep side pocket of her velvet gown. Jimmy moved so he was blocking Madame Sonya's view of Amy if she came back too soon. Sliding the compartment shut Amy placed the box where Madame Sonya had left it.

Amy heard her yelling at some poor girl. "Stupid girl, you, stupid girl! I tell you when I push button, bell ring, you come!" Amy could hear Marta trying to calm Madame Sonya. There was a bit of talk. "Idiota, get salt and water! Yes, you get now!" There was more talk. "Yes, you stupid cow, salt like you put on your stupid potatoes!"

Jimmy was still next to Amy, patting her back and acting the part of a panicked friend.

Madame Sonya finally returned with a glass of water and a shot glass of what looked like salt that she quickly added to the glass. Thank goodness, she thought, the girl was still coughing and not dead.

Amy didn't see any way out so she drank it. She felt like throwing up. She was sure she looked very ill, indeed.

Madame Sonya was grateful the awful coughing had stopped. She smiled brightly at Jimmy. "You good Doctor. Now we go!"

Amy was hoarse from all the coughing but was careful to say "Thank you. You saved my life." A little flattery never hurt and who knows, she thought, it might come in handy later.

They followed Madame Sonya, who was carefully carrying the box, out of the library. Amy knew, as soon as she was alone, Madame Sonya was going to Room 306 to put the box back where she had found it. The woman was superstitious. Amy smiled.

"Jimmy, would you like to take a walk and look at the water?" She whispered in a fake hoarse voice.

Are you crazy? It's storming outside. "Actually, I'm not feeling well. I think I'm going back to my room. I was so worried about your allergy attack that I now have a headache."

They headed up the stairs to the second floor.

"Oh, my poor friend, do take care of yourself."

Jimmy glared at her. "I will try. You are such a dear heart to worry about me."

They started walking down the long hallway that led to their rooms. Silently they were talking up a storm.

Jimmy, do you know what I think?

No, and I don't really care.

That is not nice!

I was just kidding, Amy! Honestly I was just kidding. I'm absolutely dying to know what you think...about what?

About the séance fiasco tonight...

What about it?

I think she ended it because we were strangers who didn't come here because we believed their hocus pocus but because our boat died and the winds carried us here. I am sure she does not want the other guests to think she's a con artist.

You're right about that.

"Jimmy, have a nice sleep and I'll see you for breakfast in the morning."

"I'll be outside your door at eight. Please be on time." "OK."

"Could I have a glass of water?"

"Don't you have water in your room?"

"A carafe and water is only provided in the luxury suite." Jimmy smiled sweetly.

"Come in." Amy narrowed her eyes at him as he flounced past her.

Amy was happy to see the entire contents of her small valise had been washed, dried and now folded neatly on the top of her bed. She filled a glass from her bedside carafe.

"Be sure and check that your things are back, clean and dry? Mine are." *I hate making small talk but I'm sure we're being recorded and probably filmed, too.*

"Then mine must be, too! Goodnight." *I'm sure only privileged guests, who are lucky enough to have a suite, have their laundry done for them. What do you want to bet my stuff is wet, smelly and still in my backpack?*

It took ten seconds for Jimmy to cross the hall and open the door to his room.

"Amy!!" He yelled loud enough to wake everyone on the second floor.

Amy opened her door and hissed at him. "What?"

"Could you please come over here?"

"Why?"

"Just come over here before I start screaming."

"Geez! Maybe you haven't noticed but you ARE screaming! Shut up. I'll be right there."

Jimmy was standing near the window pointing up the wall when she walked in.

"What is that?" He pointed to a thin stream of thick black liquid that went from the ceiling down the wall where it was starting to puddle on the hardwood floor.

"I believe it's called a wall."

"That's not funny. What's the stuff coming DOWN the wall?"

"This castle is like four hundred years old. Isn't it lovely?"

"It's black mold. I refuse to die of black mold in a four hundred year old castle."

"Good for you. But you have to expect some little imperfections. I told you the place is old. You wouldn't even have recognized it if the wall around it had been painted a different color."

"Like what...black to match the mold."

"I'm telling you I just know this isn't the bad type."

"So what are you? A black mold expert?" He glared at her.

Trying to change the subject. "Jimmy, isn't it exciting that you're probably sleeping in a bed that Christopher Columbus slept in on his way to discovering the New World?"

"No, I feel no flutter of excitement. He should have turned right around when he saw the ugly black mold and sailed right back to Spain."

"He wasn't from Spain. He was from Italy. He sailed under the Spanish flag. You had a misspent youth. Didn't you read any history books?"

"Obviously not as much as you did, Ms. Encyclopedia Britannica!"

"I'm going to bed. Goodnight."

Jimmy ran around wringing his hands. "Oh, sure, leave your old friend Jimmy here to rot and die."

Amy laughed. "You are such a Drama Queen, I can't believe it!"

"I am not!"

"Then go to sleep. If you last until the morning you get a surprise breakfast, remember?" Aren't you excited about that?"

"NO! Because, dear heart, if I die of black mold I won't be eating it anyway!"

Amy turned and headed for the door. "Ok, grumpy, grumpy, see you tomorrow."

Amy could still hear him grumbling as she crossed the hall, went into her room and shut the door behind her.

Amy, lock your door. We're not at the Montleone!"

Turning, she locked her door and went to bed. She had a big smile on her face. Some things just never change.

CHAPTER SEVEN

Exploring Castle Island

The next morning, Amy removed the treasure map she had pilfered last night from the secret compartment in Madame Sonya's carved box. She had placed it under her pillow which she now transferred to the pocket of her jeans. She didn't know if they were crude enough to have secret cameras in the guest bedrooms but no way was she going to leave the map in the room. She had memorized the one the sisters had given her so before she left the police station she gave Chief Barker a sealed envelope with all the information on Bugs. She was careful to dress in layers of warmth but she was still cold. The whole island was covered with a mist and a light rain, making the outside temperature dive into the 40's which was unusual for Florida in the late spring but nothing about this place was usual anyway.

Amy checked the time. It was a little after eight o'clock. She crossed the room and opened the door knowing Mr. On Time would be standing there pointing to his watch. And he was.

Amy patted him on the cheek. "Oh my goodness, you made it through the night!

"I was lucky!"

"Not all black mold is the bad kind. Most is just harmless. That stuff on your wall was harmless."

"Oh, wow, thanks so much for telling me ten hours after the fact. I could have used that little bit of information last night."

"See what comes from reading science books."

Jimmy rolled his eyes. "Let's go! I survived the night in a mold filled room because I wanted the surprise breakfast. I'm hungry. Can we please get going?"

Amy tried to look serious. "We better hurry. They could be downstairs gobbling up all the good food, Jimmy."

Amy rushed past him in the hallway, smiling.

"I never thought of that." Jimmy did a fast walk behind Amy. "That would be terrible!" Then he realized she was kidding when she turned and had a huge smile on her face. "You are tormenting me!"

"I wouldn't let that happen to you. I called down and told them that you were very excited about the great food. I asked them to make sure no one ate your portion of the surprise breakfast."

"Awww, thanks. That was really nice. You did that for me, Amy?"

"NO, I did NOT!"

"You can be Miss Meany when you want to be." Jimmy said this while looking down at the carpeted stairs. Going up was easy but going down required tactical maneuvering. It was so easy to trip.

Margaret was holding two seats next to her when Amy and Jimmy finally made it to the dining room. All the guests were there except for them.

Jimmy narrowed his eyes at Amy when he noticed just about all the dishes on the buffet table were empty. *See. I told you. We're late and there's nothing left.*

Amy smiled and sat down next to Margaret. "Was it good?" Amy smiled.

"In just a second the staff will bring out more plates and replenish the buffet table."

Jimmy, dear, sit down. Food is on its way!"

True to what she said Marta brought out plates they placed in front of Amy and Jimmy. This was followed by the rest of the kitchen staff carrying platters of biscuits with white sausage gravy, Eggs Benedict, plus a variety of other egg dishes, grilled tomatoes, link sausages, small pancakes with butter, little bottles of maple syrup. Everything was placed on a marble topped mahogany sideboard against the wall. At the same time they removed all the empty serving dishes.

"You are forgiven." Jimmy mumbled as he rushed over to the heaping table. Without having to ask, a staff member brought a stepstool.

Margaret sighed. *Oh your poor dears. You must have been without food for a long time out there on the water.*

Margaret, it was only a few hours. He always eats like this.

Amy took her plate over to the sideboard. The way Jimmy was stacking his plate she wondered if there was going to be anything left. Reverend Damian walked up behind her. "The staff is very accommodating. No matter the hour, just ask."

"Thank you. That is very kind." Amy scooped up a hearty portion of scrambled eggs, bacon, sliced tomatoes and cold toast before turning to the Reverend. "Do you think I might borrow binoculars, a notebook and a pen? Unfortunately my things are still on the boat. They ended up underwater with everything else. I'd love to do some bird watching this morning. Oh, and maybe a zip lock baggie in case it starts raining.

"Of course." The Reverend waved one of his staff over and requested the items Amy asked for. "But don't forget to be back before lunch at Noon. The Murder Mystery Dinner Party is tonight.

At least I hope we will be having one. There is an approaching storm. It might just miss us at the last minute. I really hope so but one must be prepared. Just in case it's a go the forest area on the island must be free of guests for the staff to hide clues for the mystery.

"There is a lot to see but I promise to be back."

"We have fifty acres of flora and fauna."

"Oh, my. I had no idea it was so large."

They talked as they made their way down the buffet line.
"You're not going alone, are you?"

"Margaret has offered to give me a guided tour of your beautiful island."

"Indeed it is." When she got to the end of the line the Reverend handed Amy a little bag with everything she had asked for. "I added a compass. We can't lose our guests. That would not do at all. I also added some snacks and two bottles of water."

"Thank you. This is very kind of you."

When Amy got back to the table she smiled and asked Margaret, "Is the tour of the island still on?"

"Definitely! Would you like to go after breakfast?"

"I'd love to. Maybe Marsha would like to join us." She figured Marsha would decline the invitation because she looked like she was not feeling very well.

Marsha looked up from across the table. "Not me, Amy. I'm a bit under the weather."

"I understand." While Margaret was talking to Marsha across the dining room table Amy quickly finished her breakfast.

Amy and Margaret were headed out the front door of the tower room when Jimmy raced up behind them. "Me, too. I want to see everything. What's in the bag?"

Amy laughed and ruffled his bright red hair, which stuck up straight in the back no matter how much patting down he did every morning. "Nothing much. Binoculars, a notebook, stuff like that."

They walked single file through the dense forest. Amy commented on the beauty of the tropical plants.

Margaret knew the name for each one. To Amy's delight she was a book of knowledge.

"The White Bird of Paradise is lovely." *When we get to the waterfall suggest we relax on the big flat rock beside the waterfall. The sound of the water in the background is the only place on the island where we are not heard or observed.*

Thank goodness it's safe somewhere.

When they got to the waterfall Amy understood what Margaret meant. The waterfall was about a hundred feet high and very loud.

Amy raised her voice to be heard. "I'd love to lay on the big rock over there. I could use a nap after that hike."

Margaret answered immediately. "Me, too."

Jimmy looked at the dark lagoon water. "I brought a book to read and a nap would be great...from right here under this tree." He raised his voice and shouted at Amy. "Especially needed since I didn't get any sleep last night worrying about the deadly black mold growing on the wall in my bedroom! Right, AMY!"

Amy clucked in sympathy. "You poor dear. It was hit or miss but you made it through the night. It's a miracle, I tell you, a real miracle."

"Well you and your friend go hoping around on rocks. For my part I'm going to stay right here on solid ground. Oh, Amy dear, do watch out for alligators and water snakes."

Amy smiled at the thought. Taking out the notebook, pen and binoculars she left the bag with Jimmy. "Leave something for us."

"Wow, thanks!" Jimmy lost no time finding the snacks.

"For your information alligators and water snakes do not hop up on rocks!" She knew there weren't any alligators or water snakes in this small pond. At least she hoped that was true. Hopping from the shore to a series of rocks Amy and Margaret made their way to the big flat rock next to the waterfall.

"How do you know? Jimmy grinned. "I read that for a tasty treat they have been recorded doing just that."

Amy laughed. "I'll keep you posted, Jimmy dear."

The girls sat on the rock. Amy understood why not even a good listening device could pick up any sound over the thunder of the waterfall. But just in case she said, "This is such a relaxing place I think I'll take a nap." Amy lay back and closed her eyes. *I came to Ravensclaw looking for a client's nephew. His name is Bugs Robichaux. He disappeared a year ago. Bugs inherited this island. Damian was living here as a tenant. Bugs supposedly sold the Reverend the house and the island. I checked with the Police. All the paperwork was in order. Bugs sold it to Damian for cash. Bugs was on his way back to Key West to deposit the money in a bank but he never made it. Bugs and the money disappeared. I'm also looking for a girl. Her name is Frankie. She left Key West with Damian to go to Ravensclaw on the offer of a job. It's too coincidental that two people disappeared after being with Damian.*

Margaret pulled out a book from her backpack and started reading. *I have something to tell you. I went to school with two Robichaux girls.* "I think I'll read, do you mind?"

"I think reading is a great idea. I'll bring a book next time."

That school you went to...it wouldn't be Dominican, would it?

Yes, the Robichaux sisters, Lynne and Gayle, were in my class.

Small world, Margaret. "I'm going to rest. I'm not used to so much walking."

If there were any cameras they appeared to be two women, not talking but enjoying the morning, one reading, and one laying, with her eyes closed, on a large flat rock. It was surprisingly warm. Amy was glad she had worn layers of clothes which were easy to take off.

Margaret turned a page and started silently talking. *Ray and I arrived this past Friday, very late in the afternoon. Saturday morning I went exploring and found this pond. The next day, this past Sunday, I went for my morning walk. This time I brought my bathing suit and swam behind the waterfall for a quick look around. I could hear a man and a woman talking somewhere nearby. They were talking about being held captive somewhere in a dungeon. There is a walkable ledge but only for a short distance. The cavern is* about six feet high but to the left, as it goes further into the cave, the ceiling slopes underwater. I wanted to leave and go to the Police but Ray said we had told the Reverend how excited we were about coming to Ravensclaw for the Murder Mystery. If we wanted to leave early the Reverend might find that strange. We made plans to leave right after the event and go straight to the Key West Police.

Amy turned over on her stomach. I feel certain it must be Bugs and Frankie. There has to be a cave opening from the ocean side.

Margaret turned a page in her book. Yes, but I've never seen it. Dr. Lowery's husband had made plans to go fishing yesterday. Before breakfast I secretly handed him a note and asked him to discreetly check out a cave on that side, possibly underwater, above the boat house, and let me know. Then you and Jimmy arrived. Last night at dinner his wife gave me a note telling me a cave opening was definitely there but it was underwater. You could only find it if you were looking for it.

Amy again turned over and lay on her back, shielding her eyes from the dappled sunlight through the trees. You and Ray came here for something besides the Murder Mystery, didn't you?

Margaret was careful to turn the pages of her book at regular intervals. We were in Key West when a couple we know said the

Reverend and his wife were con artists. They had come to Ravensclaw for a séance with the promise that their dear daughter would appear and they would know she was safe and happy but Madame Sonya cancelled. She said she couldn't connect with her spiritual guide because there was a horrendous rain storm over the island. They said they were encouraged to stay and wait for a better night. Of course they had to pay the Reverend. Then a week later, when they had the séance once again, the Reverend had another excuse. He said he was very sorry but the stars were not in the right alignment that night. Our friends left. The Reverend said since it was their choice to leave they forfeited the money they had given him.

Wow! Like last night. Did you know I recognized Marsha and her husband from a Murder Mystery at a Plantation in Louisiana?

Oh yes, Devereux. Marsha told me she and her husband work for an internet paranormal website. They go around looking to expose fake haunted places and then write about it on the web. She has some interesting stories.

I wondered about them. I think it's time to call my Dolphin friends for a helping hand.

I can't wait to see this.

Amy silently sent out an SOS distress call to Melody.

In a short time she heard Melody calling. *I brought Harp with me. We're at the dock. Where are you?*

Go pass the boathouse and start looking for an underwater cave. Follow it inside to a waterfall.

It was just a short time and Amy heard Melody calling out. *Okay. We're behind the waterfall.*

Don't come into the lagoon. There are cameras all over the place. Can you follow the water and tell me where it goes?

Right on it, Amy.

It seemed like ages before she heard from the Dolphins.

Amy, you

there? Yes.

We ended up in a big cave. There were two people sitting at a table playing cards. I heard the man call the woman Frankie.

Melody, tell me about the name. Is he tall and wears glasses?

Yes and the woman called Frankie called him Bugs.

I've been looking for them. They were kidnapped. Are they okay?

More than okay. They have lots of huge bottles of water, and tons of canned food. They were talking about something called MRE's.

Those are Meals Ready to Eat. Can they swim out the way you came in?

Not unless they're really fish in disguise.

Melody, would you carry a message for me to the Marina in Key West. You have to find my friend, Harry, he owns the boat, Gone Fishing, in slip #12, or find Paulo, he owns the Marina Store. I'm going to give you a message. Bring it to Harry or Paulo.

Will do.

Wait. I'll write the message.

Amy looked in the bag with the supplies the Reverend had given her. She pulled out the notebook and a pen. She looked through the binoculars and then quickly wrote a note and slipped it into a zip lock baggie the Reverend had thoughtfully provided.

Amy turned to Margaret. *I have to find a way to toss this behind the waterfall.*

Amy, I have an idea. I'll point to a tree and get really excited. You jump up and look through the binoculars and gesture wildly at the tree, then shout for me to look at something. You make a big deal out of seeing something. Anyone watching the cameras will have their attention diverted to you. Call it some rare exotic bird in this area or something. I'll discreetly grab the bag and jump in the water. It will look natural for me since I've been swimming in the lagoon before.

Amy jumped up and yelled while she pointed to a tree quite close to where Jimmy was sitting. "Look! Look! It's a Red Marled Rotterroutter! Jimmy, look it's in the next tree over!"

Jimmy leaped up, playing his part every well. "Oh, wow! Oh, wow! Fantastic!"

Margaret slipped off the rock and into the water. She swam underwater behind the waterfall. She immediately saw the Dolphins. She threw the watertight sealed bag and one of the Dolphins snatched it in her mouth and then they both took off.

Returning, Margaret sat back on the rock and opened her book.

"Do you always swim in your clothes?"

Margaret laughed. "Only when I'm overly warm. It's a great way to cool off."

"Well, you just missed it. There was a Red Marled Rotterroutter in the tree! It's a rare bird, only found in the Caribbean."

"How exciting! I'm really starting to love this bird watching. Listen I think we have a little more time to explore the island before we have to return for lunch. The Reverend wants everyone inside while they leave clues in the forest for the Murder Mystery."

"It certainly sounds like great fun!" Amy put a lot of enthusiasm into her voice. What she wanted to do was rescue Bugs and Frankie and get away from here.

"The Reverend is known for his incredible Murder Mysteries! And he's quite handsome, isn't he?" *A little praise is a good idea since he's probably been watching you and Jimmy like a hawk.*

"Oh, yes, he is!" *Good move. I bet right this minute he's salivating over the monitor, watching us.*

Reverend Damian turned away from the monitor. He was delighted to be spoken of so highly. He was now sure the new guests were no threat, he would review the rest of the tape later. Right now he had to oversee lunch and make sure his staff knew where to put the clues for the Murder Mystery. It was a shame he was abandoning the island when they left tomorrow for Key West but he knew when to get out and the time was now. He had made plans months ago. During the Pirate Fest, while everyone was occupied, he would gas up his boat and he and his family would head for the Bahamas. A float plane would first pickup Sonya and his girls, then he would sink his boat before joining them. He had a private jet waiting in the

Bahamas to take them back to their home in Romastia in Eastern Europe. He had enough cash and jewels, stolen from guests over the last five years, so his family could live in luxury for the rest of their lives. He had a letter ready to mail from the Bahamas to the Key West Police telling them where to find Bugs and Frankie. By the time the Police Chief got it he would be home back in the family castle in Romastia where he was known by his family name, Count Loric. Before he came to Key West he had a royal title without any money. But now things had changed. Thanks to gullible guests he could affect repairs to his castle and stock his forest with game for hunting. Oh, yes, life was wonderful.

"We have to be on time for lunch." Amy checked her watch, and looking back she gave Jimmy an encouraging smile so he would keep up.

"Don't act smiley with me! All this jungle exploring sure has made you girls hungry!" Jimmy grumbled as he speed walked to keep up with the girls, as he called them.

"The Reverend made a special point that we had to be back so the staff has time to put clues in the jungle. Part of the Murder Mystery."

A clap of thunder almost blocked out what she was saying. "Wow! We are we in for a big storm!"

Margaret flinched as the skies darkened and lightning flashed nearby. "I heard Dr. Lowery talking about a hurricane. But I'm from New Orleans. We're used to them."

"I've never been in a hurricane before."

Jimmy jumped in with his opinion of the evening ahead. "Have your raincoats ready!" *The Murder Mystery, if it's anything like the Reverend, will probably be boring and I'll also be amazed if just one event he has planned comes through. I think a storm would be more exciting.*

Amy smiled brightly. "Sounds like great fun! I can't wait!"

"I'd rather sleep." Jimmy grumbled.

Amy turned and glared at him. "Jimmy, if you're going to be a party pooper, then just go do something else when the Murder Mystery starts."

"I might just do that!" Jimmy squirmed out of her reach when she turned around again.

"Fine!" Amy turned and stared straight ahead.

"Fine!" Jimmy fussed all the way back to the house and into the dining room.

Once again they were the last to arrive. Margaret quickly explained to everyone that they were having so much fun they lost track of time. Then, to cover their tracks, she began an engaging story about the rare bird they saw. The staff entered the dining room in single file carrying silver serving dishes they placed on the sideboard. Margaret picked up a plate and waited her turn in the buffet line.

Amy returned the binoculars and the compass to the Reverend who appeared eager to talk to her.

"Miss Amy, dear lady, your bird guide called." He kept his voice low. "He said he secured another boat for the rest of the tour and he would be at the dock at ten tomorrow morning. He said he would be taking you and Jimmy to Bird Island."

"Brilliant!" Amy smiled at the Reverend.

"By good fortune our plans were to also leave tomorrow morning right after breakfast for Key West. Are you sure you don't want to go with us? We will be staying at a very grand hotel."

Amy conjured up the most forlorn look she could muster. "And miss Bird Island? Reverend Damian, you know how I love bird watching. I can't miss it. Later, after we get our fill of rare and exotic birds, we will join you in Key West. I take it this pirate event will be on for a bit?"

"Yes, it starts on Friday and lasts for two weeks."

"Well, there you are. I'm sure we'll be back in time for at least a few days at the end."

"Before we leave tomorrow I'll give you information on where we will be staying. I'm sure the Blue Dolphin will have extra rooms if you change your mind."

"You are so kind." Amy turned back to the feast laid out on the buffet sideboard.

Delicious hamburgers on sesame buns, French fries and a choice of condiments was on the menu. Halfway through the meal Reverend Damian had the staff turn on all the lights. It was turning darker and darker outside. Rain beat down on the mullioned windows. Wind bent the trees back and forth. Limbs closest to the house swept against the stone mansion and brushed the windows. Amy was thankful that Ravensclaw ran on a huge bank of generators so there was no chance of losing power.

Finally over dessert Reverend Damian returned to the dining room and read off a series of announcements. "We just heard over the radio that this storm is moving very slowly and we are right in its path. It would be folly to hold a Murder Mystery since the venue has always been outside. So I have changed the program. But first a few more announcements. Amy's bird guide called so Amy and Jimmy will not leave with us for Key West after breakfast. They will be picked up on the dock at ten in the morning. For everyone else we will----"

Margaret stood up and addressed Reverend Damian. "---I would love to go to Bird Island. If Amy will let us join her tour, Ray and I would be delighted."

Amy was thrilled. She didn't want her friend to get on the boat with the Reverend. Standing, she made sure she was heard. "Reverend Damian, of course Margaret and her husband are welcome to join us. So that makes four less in your boat."

Dr. Lowery called out. "Reverend Damian, we have our own boat so the four in our party will also be leaving in the morning. Quite early, actually. I think the men plan on a little fishing before we get to the hotel."

Marsha quickly added. "I have friends who are coming to pick Mark and I up in the morning. We will meet at the hotel in Key West."

Reverend Damian was doing his best not to look aggravated. "I'm sorry to see everyone going in different directions but it does give us more room in our boat. I am taking the entire staff to Key West to enjoy the Pirate Fest. Lady Catherine and Miranda, you are still coming with us?"

"Yes. We will leave with you in your boat. We can't wait to get to the hotel and see the famous Pirate Festival." Lady Catherine graciously waved to the other guests. "We'll see you there, everyone."

"I am very pleased we have that organized. After lunch please go directly to the library. Madame Sonya and Marta will set up our giant theater screen and present two thrilling horror movies for our guests. While everyone is enjoying the movies the staff will prepare a final dinner. For our English guests we plan on roast beef, mushy peas, and Yorkshire pudding. For our Southern guests we will be offering Southern fried chicken, mashed potatoes and gravy, and corn pudding. Desserts will be rice pudding and mini pecan pies. Dinner will be at eight this evening. Thank you for understanding our change in plans."

The guests were all speaking at once. Some were talking about which movies had been chosen for them to watch, some were talking about the storm, others were talking about getting packed to leave after breakfast in the morning and everyone was talking about the incredible dinner the Reverend had planned.

"I LOVE mushy peas!" Jimmy was ecstatic.

"Well, isn't that nice for you!" Amy wondered what he didn't like.

"I'll save us seats in the Library." Jimmy fast walked out of the room.

Amy and Margaret weren't being nosy but they couldn't miss the conversation between Lady Catherine and her ladies maid, Miranda, since they were right behind them going out of the dining room.

"I am NOT watching a stupid horror movie! I have a horrible headache. I am going to crash until we eat." Miranda kept her voice low.

"Could you just show up and then split?" Lady Catherine hissed.

"No! Stop harassing me!"

Lady Catherine, realizing that Amy and Margaret were behind them changed her voice from backwoods Tennessee to London central. "Oh, yes, I understand. Do take a nap. I'll see you at dinner then."

The conversation ended. Lady Catherine headed for the Library and Miranda stomped off for the guest bedrooms on the second floor.

Wow! From the way Miranda barks out orders one would think it's Lady Miranda and her ladies maid, Catherine. And by the way that pair are not from England. They just dropped their accent completely. They sound more like Hillbillies!

Amy, you are too funny. I noticed that, too.

How long have they been at Ravensclaw?

From what I overheard they have been here for quite a while. Lady Catherine said she feels closest to her daughter here. She told everyone she lost her daughter in a tragic accident in Cornwall.

Oh, baloney. I could just bet that the only Cornwall they've ever heard about is Cornwall, Tennessee.

CHAPTER EIGHT

A Very Scary Movie

They arrived at the library. They couldn't miss Jimmy waving from the front row. He was sitting in one chair and had his hands on the chairs to his right and left. Amy and Margaret hurried to take their seats. He moved over so the girls could sit next to each other and talk.

"Margaret, what about your husband?"

"He went fishing with the guys this morning. They just returned. I left him in the room soaking wet. They were caught in the storm. The Reverend sent lunch to the rooms."

Amy tried to look impressed. "Room service, no less."

"First class place." Margaret grinned.

"Ladies, ladies, and gentlemen, can I have your attention, please!" Marta called out.

Amy was amazed at her grasp of English.

The lights and candles were all extinguished in the large room.

Marta continued her introduction to the movies they were going to watch. "The first movie is titled **Invasion of the Body**

Snatchers. It's about aliens who grow pods that produce exact replicas of the person they are going to replace. The setting is a small fishing village somewhere in the Pacific Northwest. The second movie is **Night of the Living Dead.** It's about zombies who trap some people in a farmhouse. Please feel free to scream out if you wish!"

At that moment lightning cracked outside. There was a fierce moaning sound as the wind intensified its thrashing through the trees, smashing their limbs ever so close to the ancient and delicate multi paned windows. Everyone screamed.

"Wow! The movie hasn't even started." Jimmy looked around amazed at the fear a little bit of lighting could bring out in the guests.

Marta started the projector and the credits for the first movie rolled. The wind drove the rain, hitting the windows in a vertical direction. The storm was so loud outside that Marta had to turn up the sound on the movie machine.

Jimmy, for all of his bravado, sat in his seat absolutely petrified by the pods that looked more like giant watermelons. For once he wished he hadn't gone to sleep earlier by the waterfall. He was not at all sleepy right now and to get up and leave was out of the question. He did not want to look like a big baby. He gripped the arms of his chair and closed his eyes. Somehow that made him feel a bit better. That is until they started watching the second movie with the zombies. He gripped Amy's arm.

"Jimmy, would you let go of me! You need to relax. Try a little meditation."

"Oh, right, and I guess you think those poor people trapped in that farmhouse are meditating right this very minute?"

"No, I think they're actors and they're praying that they can get through this acting job without laughing. Try doing that? And by the way you were acting so brave during the pod people movie. I thought you'd scream at some point."

"I am not a baby. I never scream!" Jimmy went back to gripping his chair. Amy was being Miss Meany again. Just wait until she was scared about something. Just wait! But he couldn't think of anything that would scare her. By the time he finished reflecting on his plight in life the movie ended. Jimmy breathed a sigh of relief and hopped off his chair. "I'll see you at dinner. I'm going to take a shower. I hope the mold in my room hasn't taken over the shower, too."

Amy and Margaret stood up. "We're leaving, too."

Jimmy stood to one side while the girls left the library. "What mold?" Margaret looked worried.

Jimmy, walking behind them, used his scary voice. "That's the next movie on the agenda. I call it **Murder of the Guests by the Mold People!** He gave out with a maniacal laugh.

Amy looked at Margaret and rolled her eyes. "That is not nice to scare someone, Jimmy."

"Well just how would you feel? You don't care that I've have mold growing on my bedroom wall."

"How awful! Can I look at it? I know something about mold."

"Margaret, I would love that. Thank you!" He looked at Amy. "At least some people care if I die of bad black mold."

They headed down the hallway to their rooms. Jimmy opened his door and to his surprise the mold was gone. "I can't believe it. No more gross mold."

"Well good, Jimmy. That's taken care of. See you all at dinner." Margaret waved as she walked down the hallway towards her room.

Amy looked at her friend and ruffled his hair. "I'm sorry about that mold. I'm glad it's gone. I knew it wasn't the bad kind. I used to read about various molds in the library growing up. We had some in the laundry room and I had the job of cleaning it up."

"Well, why didn't you say something!" Jimmy sniffled then went into his room and shut the door.

Amy smiled when she heard a chair being dragged across the room and wedged under the door handle. She undressed and took off the jade heart One Eyed and Jocko had given her on Treasure Island. It was very precious to her. Her Dad had bought it for her birthday but the cruise accident happened before he could give it to her. She hid it behind the small clock on her end table. Turning on the water she pinned her hair on top of her head before stepping into the extra-large tub in her bathroom. She couldn't wait to take a little nap before dinner. It seemed like she had just closed her eyes when her clock alarm went off. She quickly dressed in the velvet gown from the night before.

Ready for dinner Jimmy opened his door. There were no sounds coming from Amy's room across the hall. He dragged out the small ladder that had been left in his room, closed his door, blew out the gas light in the hall, and banged on Amy's door before quickly moving away.

He could hear movement from inside her room. Amy threw open the door and stepped into the hall.

Someone very tall, wearing a long robe, was outlined in the darkness. She couldn't see who it was, he was standing stiff legged, arms raised and straight ahead. She could just make out someone with his tongue hanging out the side of his mouth. The demented looking person made horrible gurgling sounds.

Amy stood there transfixed with her mouth open. It looked like one of the zombies from the movie had taken over somebody's body. She let out a strangled sob. Turning, she raced back inside her room and slammed the door, locking it securely.

"Amy, dear, are you okay?" Jimmy grinned.

"Did you see that horrible zombie in the hall?" Any spoke through her closed door.

"No, I didn't. Maybe your screaming scared the awful thing away." He couldn't hold it in any longer, he started laughing.

Amy threw her door open. "You little rat, that was you! How did you get so tall?"

"Well, someone left a ladder in my room. I guess it was when they cleaned the mold."

Amy saw the humor of it all and started laughing. "Okay, you got me!" She left her room and followed Jimmy down the hall. She glared at the offending ladder as they went by.

Jimmy smiled all the way down the stairs to the dining room. Everyone was beautifully dressed. Amy admired the beautiful ruby and diamond necklace that Lady Catherine was wearing. It was accompanied by a matching ruby and diamond ring. The diamonds surrounding the rubies were blinding. Amy noticed the Reverend was also very interested in Lady Catherine. He sat her to his right and devoured her with his eyes.

Amy sat next to Margaret. They were both staring at the jewels. *Wow! Must be family heirlooms.*

Margaret studied the menu for the evening that had been placed across her plate. *Before you arrived she told us that very thing. It seems that when her mother died she inherited the family jewels. Her brother inherited everything else.*

Amy studied her menu and glanced with interest at the sideboard filled with covered silver serving dishes waiting for the staff to bring each one around. *Oh, yes. The English do have that oldest boy inherits the title and everything rule.*

He didn't get the jewels! Very true.

Margaret and Amy's attention was taken by the wonderful things being offered by the staff.

Amy was always amazed by the amount of food Jimmy consumed. When they were finished eating and the plates were removed by the staff, the Reverend called for attention.

"Breakfast tomorrow morning will be early at seven. Have your bags outside your door before you come down and the staff will take everything to the tower room. For those who are not ready to go to sleep the projector is set up in the library. Just tell Marta what gruesome horror movie you'd like to see if you dare!" He laughed and checked his watch. "It's almost ten. So I will see all of you in the morning. This has been a very long day."

Everyone milled about in the hall.

Amy yawned. "I'm going to sleep."

"I still have to pack. I'll see you tomorrow." Margaret waved and headed for the staircase.

"Jimmy, which way are you going?"

"To pack."

They walked up the stairs to their rooms. Jimmy hauled the stepladder back into his room and shut the door.

A storm raged outside but inside it was snug and warm. Amy threw more logs on the open fire in her bedroom. There was just something exciting about a rain storm outside and a warm fire inside. She quickly fell asleep.

She woke up early to a dripping sound as runoff rain slid down the slate roof to the ground. Sometime earlier the storm had passed over the island and headed out to sea. It was six in the morning. With great difficulty she left her warm bed to finish packing and get dressed. Since the Reverend and his staff were leaving for Key West right after breakfast the staff was busy in the hall carrying bags down the stairs.

Not forgetting her jade heart she moved her small alarm clock to retrieve the treasure she had hidden before she took her bath last night. It wasn't there! Amy frantically looked behind the end table, under the bed, behind the bed. It was gone. She remembered very clearly placing it behind her clock on the bedside table, well hidden from view. She calmed down for a minute to think. The staff had keys to all the rooms. When she was not in the room all the staff had access to her room as did the guests. The door only locked from the inside so when she went down to dinner the door was unlocked, as was every guest door. There was little she could do because it could have been anyone. She made one last check, this time behind the end table, and there it was. It must have fallen. She quickly slid it over her head. It felt so good to be back against her warm skin.

Jimmy knocked lightly on the door. He was carrying his backpack.

"I thought someone had taken my jade heart. I always wear it except when I bathe. Thank goodness I found it on the floor!"

"I lost something and it wasn't on the floor."

"What happened?"

"Someone lifted me gold dust, which is very upsetting. That person also took me lucky gold coin me Mum gave me before I left Ireland."

"Oh, Jimmy, I'm so sorry! Maybe we'll get lucky and find out who did it and we will take it back!"

"Plan on it."

The rest of the walk into the dining room was very gloomy.

Breakfast was hastily thrown together with egg and ham sandwiches, a fruit cup and a glass of orange juice. Amy was thrilled at the thought of finding Bugs and Frankie and most of all seeing Harry. She thought about him and wondered if he was feeling the same for her. She'd soon find out.

At nine the doorbell sounded and in walked a couple who had come to pick up Marsha and Mark. The staff made sure they were given a bag of sandwiches to go. After all the goodbyes they left to board their friend's boat tied up at the dock.

At nine-thirty the rest of the guests were waiting on the dock while the staff was rushing around closing up the house.

Dr. Lowery and Delta, waited patiently while the husbands brought their fishing boat to the dock to pick them up.

Amy waved goodbye to everyone and prayed Harry would be on time. Jimmy made sure Amy's valise was on the dock. Ray did the same for his and Margaret's leather luggage.

The Reverend brought his fifty foot pink and white yacht to the dock so Sonya, the staff, Lady Catherine and Miranda could board! Amy politely coughed to hide a laugh. Who has a pink and white boat?

With all their luggage and staff below deck the Reverend checked his watch. Lady Catherine and Miranda sat in chairs looking bored.

"Reverend Damian, really, no need to wait on us. My guide will be here. Why don't you just get on your way? We'll be fine."

"No, no! We never leave a guest behind!" He had a wicked laugh over that. He raised a hand to shield his eyes. "I do believe I see a boat coming this way. That must be your guide. It looks like uh...um...a lobster boat."

"Yes, It is. Now, you can leave. I don't want to make you late getting to the hotel."

"No, no. Don't you mind?" A very awkward silence followed until Harry and Joey were within shouting distance.

"Ahoy, mates." Joey shouted out as they drew closer. "We're here to save the day and take you on to Bird Island."

Harry appeared from the small cabin below. *I am really glad to see you!*

"I have friends joining us. This is Margaret and Ray. Margaret is a fellow bird watcher."

While they were making small talk Jimmy tossed the cast off lines to the Reverend who secured them and powered up his boat. "He's off with waves all around."

"Bye for now. See you at the Blue Dolphin Hotel." Jimmy called out.

Amy, Jimmy and her friends, got on Harry's borrowed boat. He was busy at the wheel but not too busy to give Amy a lingering look and a smile.

Jimmy cast off and they eagerly got away from the island, going in the opposite direction from the Reverend who was making good time on his way to Key West.

"Whew!" Amy unclenched her hands. "Oh, Harry. I am so happy to see you!" Joey came topside. "Hey, Joey! Margaret and Ray know all about Bugs and Frankie. I think it's time for me to call Dolphin Rescue!" She was silent for a moment while she looked out at the surprisingly calm ocean. *Melody, we need your help. Harry's here. The Reverend has gone. We're turning back to the Island now. Can you bring a friend? See you at the dock.*

We hear you, Amy. On our way!

"They're coming. Harry, how's the "Gone Fishing?""

"Still in repairs. We were lucky to get this boat. It's not fast, but it floats."

"That's the most important part! Thank you for rescuing us."

"At your service." *I want to give you a big hug right now but we have to get Bugs and Frankie out of that dungeon before the Reverend changes his mind and comes back.*

Amy blushed.

Melody and a Dolphin Amy hadn't seen before leaped out of the water.

Amy, this is my friend Lindy! She's visiting. She is very eager to help. Grande was a little too large to get through to the kids. I tease him about it now.

Margaret was watching the interaction between them. "Margaret, that's Melody and she has a friend, Lindy, with her. Lindy is from out of town. Melody, and her friends, gave us a tow to the island." The graceful Dolphins leaped and splashed in the water.

Follow us, Amy. They leaped together and took off like grey rockets in the water.

Harry followed. In minutes they were outside the underwater entrance to the cave. Harry turned off the engines and released the anchor. Joey brought up four scuba tanks on deck and was busy carefully checking each one and all the gear.

Melody, would you go see if that couple is still there? Sure enough. Be right back.

Harry took that time to go over how to run the boat in case Ray and Margaret had to get out of there fast. Hopefully the Reverend was well on his way to Key West and not returning to Ravensclaw.

Melody and Lindy did flips when they returned. *They're there. It's a go! Amy, what are the plans?*

Harry pulled out four headlights, the kind miners wear only these were waterproof, from a storage bench. "Joey and I will each bring one person with us."

Amy was silent for a moment. "Melody wants to know if you want a tow in and out or should they lead the way."

"Not a tow but how about one guide in front and one in the rear in case of any mishap."

"Good idea. Melody says if you have any problems just hold out your arm and she'll grab you and tow you out."

"Tell Melody that's a good idea."

"She heard you. You just can't hear her."

Amy glanced at Margaret. She and Ray were looking awestruck. Ray laughed and held up his hand. "We will never tell anyone. They would think we're crazy!"

Harry and Joey were suited up. With all his gear on Harry looked like a frogman! He gave her a hug and whispered against her neck. His breath was warm. "We've been so busy I didn't have time to do this before."

"I know."

I missed you, Amy Lafitte. He looked at her and his face mask steamed up.

Amy laughed. "I missed you, too."

I wish I could give you a big kiss but I'll wait until I can give you a proper one when I get back.

Amy blushed. "Just be careful." She couldn't stop blushing. She had never been kissed before, at least not romantically. There had never been much chance of a romance living at an orphanage with no boys her own age. Thinking about it, Harry wasn't a boy. He was a man in all manner of the word. She was thrilled and terrified at the same time. What was Serena going to say about Harry? She'd have to take it slow. One thing at a time.

Harry and Joey were sitting on the side of the boat with their hands over their mouthpieces, ready to fall over backwards into the water. They each carried a bag holding scuba gear for one person. Both Harry and Joey each had a small motorized object that looked like a torpedo and made keeping up with the Dolphins easy.

"Harry!" Amy gave him a thumbs up. They flipped over backwards into the water.

The guys made incredible speed holding the rocket in one hand and guided by the Dolphins. Melody led the way with Lindy in the rear.

The Reverend was pleased that they had made it to Key West in record time. As they pulled up to the dock at the Blue Dolphin Hotel he heard a gasp come from Lady Catherine.

"Is that where we are supposed to stay?" She made a terrible face.

"Dear Lady, it's quite lovely, you'll see." The staff, used to the routine, quickly secured the lines to the dock.

"It looks like a cheap motel!" Lady Catherine dabbed a lace handkerchief to her forehead.

The Reverend tried to keep his voice calm and reassuring. "Why don't we just take a stroll around and if you don't like the rooms we will leave immediately."

"That is acceptable!" She turned to Miranda and snarled, "You stay here." Then pointing a long boney finger at Marta she hissed, "And you...do not touch my bags until I decide."

"All staff, except for Marta, please go check in and find your rooms."

The Reverend took Lady Catherine on a short stroll showing her the lovely pool filled with baby toys and floating beer bottles. Lady Catherine looked like she was going to faint. Distressed, he quickly moved her away from the offending sight. He spoke glowingly of the rooms and led her over to the loveliest room at the Blue Dolphin Hotel, which is not saying much.

Lady Catherine shrieked in horror. She rushed over and lifted the mattress. Watching bed bugs scurry around made her ill. She was furious. "I will not stay in this bug infested place. I am used to Butlers and Cooks and fine things! I do not see anything lovely about this place you've talked so much about."

Reverend Damian tried calming her down but she was determined. "I have yet to speak to my beloved daughter and now you are dumping me in some substandard motel for a week."

"Lady Catherine, I have a wonderful idea. How would you like to stay on a million dollar yacht with a Butler and a Chef?"

Stopping her tirade she sounded almost calm. "That sounds better."

"I can arrange it!"

His mind was furiously working trying to devise another way of dealing with this difficult woman. He had planned on tying her up and stealing her jewels from her hotel room. By the time she was free he and Sonya would be sailing the ocean blue with two million American dollars and all the jewels he'd relieved from his guests for the past years, including Lady Catherine's fabulous rubies and diamonds. But now he had to placate her. He definitely didn't want her to call the police. He decided sometimes things change and you just have to go with the flow. He had another surprise in mind for this horrible woman and her mousy companion.

Lady Catherine fanned her face with a brochure she picked up from the bedside end table. "A million dollar yacht. Brilliant! Take me there at once."

The Reverend took Lady Catherine arm and returned to the pink and white yacht. Madame Sonya, Marta and Miranda were sitting in deck chairs. Once they were aboard Marta jumped up and cast the lines back on the boat before boarding herself.

"Where are we going? I certainly hope it's far away from this horrid place!" Lady Catherine was still irritated that she had been brought to a place with bed bugs to begin with.

"The yacht will be berthed at the Marina. And, a car and driver will be at your disposal to take you back and forth to the festivities every day. Of course we will be your guides." When he saw the stern look on her face he quickly added, "Or not! Whatever pleases you." He backed his yacht away from the dock saying a silent prayer there was a slip available. Since the Blue Dolphin hadn't worked out he had to make a quick adjustment in his plans for these two ladies. Stealing the jewels from Lady Catherine's room at the Blue Dolphin would have been an easy job and the last step in his plans before heading out in his boat for the Caribbean. Now he had to come up with a new idea and do it fast.

"That might be acceptable." Lady Catherine sat in a deck chair and waved her hand in a dismissive manner.

The Reverend bowed and stepped backward. As a last resort he could just tie up the English women and take them with him. After he blew up his boat he would leave them in a lifeboat when his rescue came to take him home to Romania. The thought of watching Lady Catherine helpless as he flew away almost made him smile.

Oh, and not to forget, he'd give her that irritating royal wave she was always giving him.

The Reverend's pink and white yacht arrived at the Marina dock in short time. Not seeing anyone about the Reverend handed Marta a credit card and ordered her to gas up the tanks, to the top. "You do know how to do that, right?"

"Of course, Reverend." Marta really had no idea but she knew better than to say that. She had seen what happened to girls the Reverend thought were stupid and useless to him.

The Reverend stepped from the boat to the dock and offered a hand to assist Lady Catherine. She tapped her reading glasses on his wrist in an arrogant manner and snorted in a way not usually expressed by a member of her class.

"I'm not much for useless strolling around."

He withdrew his hand. "Then, if you excuse me, I will be back shortly."

"Where exactly are you going?"

"I have to go to the Marina office to arrange a slip for the yacht and also to secure a butler. Marta is an excellent cook who will prepare all of your onboard meals. I will send one of my staff to run errands and do the housekeeping."

"Which yacht will I be staying on?"

"I think the one we're on right now. If you would like to look around I think you will find the accommodations to your liking."

"Do I have a choice?"

"I don't think so. All available hotels are booked. Pirate Fest starts at Noon and it's almost that time now."

Lady Catherine was clearly irritated. "This craft seems clean and with the services of a butler and cook it will be almost acceptable. Anyway, it's just for sleeping. I can force myself to bear this inconvenience."

The Reverend stood there stupefied. He had never been talked to like that.

Lady Catherine waved her lace hankie at him. "Well then get on with it if I don't have a choice. I am missing the start of the festivities and I am not happy about that!" She sat down in a deck chair looking like Queen for a Day.

"I won't be long, Lady Catherine. Not long at all."

The Reverend turned and headed for the Marina Store. He had never met a more disagreeable woman in his life. Getting rid of her would definitely be a happy moment.

Paulo had just turned the open sign on the door to closed when the Reverend walked in.

"Hello. I am sorry to be an imposition but I desperately need a slip. I have a fifty footer."

"Of course. I have to check availability but I'm sure I have one left." He checked a large book on his desk. "Yes. Slip 410 is available and it takes up to a hundred foot yacht so you have plenty of room. It has all the hookups. Would that suit you?"

"Most definitely."

Paulo pulled out a map of the Marina. "It's here." He pointed to something that looked quite far away from where they were right now.

"Could you please join us on our boat and show us the way?"

"No problem. I take credit cards. It's Five Hundred dollars a day, two week minimum. I'll discount it to Six Thousand Five Hundred."

"What?" The Reverend was blindsided.

"It is Pirate Fest and it is the last large slip I have left. I can assure you if you don't take it I will fill the spot within the hour."

"No, no, I will take it." He made his voice calm and pleasant. "Do you mind cash?"

"Cash is very welcome."

"Good. You take us to the slip. I'll pay you when we get to my boat."

"Lead the way." On the way out Paulo locked the door behind him. He decided after he got the Reverend into his slip, and collected the money, he would return to the store, and leave a note on the door with the exact time he would reopen, before he headed into town for the festivities. He looked back once and saw the yellow light flashing over the door which indicated someone was calling the Marina store. He made a note, when he returned, to check his caller ID just in case it was something he had to take care of right away.

As they walked the Reverend frantically tried to figure out how this was going to go. He'd get under way and then he'd order Paulo and the English ladies below deck to be tied up. He'd call out the special code to Sonya who would come topside with a weapon to entice them to follow his directions. He felt better now that he'd worked out a plan.

When they got to his boat the Reverend was surprised to see the deck empty except for Lady Catherine sitting in the same deck chair waving like the Queen. "Lady Catherine, this is Paulo. He'll show us to our slip and then we can go into town for the festivities. Paulo, please come aboard. I'll have one of my Staff cast off."

Lady Catherine gave Paulo a royal wave.

Paulo boarded with the Reverend right behind him.

"Sonya, Marta, where the devil are you?" The Reverend shouted.

Lady Catherine stood and pointed a gun at the Reverend. "Hey, Rev, don't do anything stupid." All pretense of an English accent was gone. At that moment Miranda joined her, armed with a very serious looking gun.

Paulo stood there with his mouth open. "Exactly what is going on? I have nothing to do with your problems with each other."

"Too late. You're part of this now." Not taking her eyes off the men she spoke quietly to Miranda. "You get on below now in case one of these here gentlemen tries anything funny and believe me, Rev, if you do, it's gonna be your last. Miranda grew up shooting with her brothers." She indicated, with her gun, that the two men go below deck. She was right behind them.

"Tie 'em up." Lady Catherine barked out orders. She snorted out a strangled laugh.

"Lady Catherine, where is my wife and Marta?" The Reverend tried to sound calm.

"In the luxurious accommodations you mentioned earlier." And it's not Lady Catherine. It's SueAnn." She laughed. "I bet I fooled ya, I sure did."

"You changed your lovely name." The Reverend was trying his best to be charming.

"Lady SueAnn just didn't cut it, if ya get my drift, Rev!"

Miranda quickly tied them up. The Reverend kept up a line of talk. "I have to complement you on your English accent. It was spot on, as they say in England." He laughed lightly.

"Why, thank ya, Sugah. I try to be professional." "You could have been in the theater you're so good."

"Why, honey, I do declare ya noticed. Enough of this inane chit-chat. Me and Miranda are just two Southern belles doing what ya do, only better. Now here's how it's going to go. Ya gonna do everything I say and ya might come out of this alive."

Miranda had just finished tying them up as SueAnn got to the end of her little speech. "Marinda, honey child, cast off and get this boat under way. And watch the speed limit!" She pointed her gun in a very unfriendly way. "Park yourselves on the sofa. Now!" She waved her gun and the Reverend moved fast. He pulled a terrified Paulo next to him.

"Where are we going?" Paulo heard the lines hitting the deck. He could feel the boat move and rightly surmised that they were drifting away from the dock. He heard the engines start up.

They were underway. If he'd just left for town earlier he wouldn't be here right now. "I'd like to know what's going on!"

"Shut up. Ya'll will know when I'm ready to tell ya." SueAnn leaned against the galley counter. She aimed her very serious big gun right at her hostages.

Bugs and Frankie were standing on the little beach wondering if they would ever get out of there when Harry and Joey popped up out of the water looking like sea creatures with scuba gear on. The Dolphins leaped up and spun around. Frankie screamed and ran for cover with Bugs right behind to protect her.

"Wait! Wait!" Harry pulled off his mask, "Frankie, you know me. I'm Harry Morgan. I have a boat at the Marina. Your brother, Paulo, is a friend of mine." He raised his voice. "Bugs, your aunts sent two private investigators, from the French Quarter, to find you."

There was furious whispering between the two who were huddled as far away as they could get from the water. They finally made a decision and approached Harry.

Frankie's voice was shaky. Harry, I do know you. You're really here to rescue us?"

"Yes, we sure are. Bugs, I don't know if you know Amy Lafitte. She and Jimmy O'Brien have a detective agency in the

French Quarter. Your aunts hired them to find you. And Frankie, your brother has never stopped looking for you. Both of you were kidnapped by the Reverend and his wife. You are in a cave under the castle."

"Why?"

"Let's get out of here. We can talk topside and we have a phone on our boat so Frankie you can call Paulo. The Reverend and his whole band of thieves have left the island."

At this moment he had never seen two people who were happier than these two. "By the way, this is Joey. The only way out of here is by scuba." He and Joey handed over the two sets of scuba gear.

"And the Dolphins?"

"They played a big part in your rescue. Amy will tell you all about it. Right now we have to get out of here before the Reverend decides to come back. Have either of you done any scuba?"

Bugs answered. "I have."

Frankie just shook her head.

"Okay, Bugs, get Frankie into her gear. Frankie, one big rule in scuba is never stop breathing. And no matter what happens don't panic. We're here to help you."

"Ok."

"We have to hurry. The Dolphins will lead front and back. We each have an underwater headlamp. The lights go on over your mask." Harry demonstrated how to put them on. "Joey and I have water rockets so we can keep up with the Dolphins. Bugs, hold onto Joey's weight belt with one hand. That leaves your other hand free to hold the regulator against your mouth. Frankie, I know you'll feel safer if you hold onto Bugs and do the same. I'll be behind you in case one of you has a problem. We're going out the way we came in. OK? Everyone ready? We'll be out of here before you know it."

If everything just went as planned it would be too easy. About halfway out Frankie brushed against the side of the cave and dislodged something that wrapped around her leg for a brief second. She screamed as best she could with a regulator in her mouth and let go of Bugs to hit at the object that was trying to get away from her at the same time. When she stopped short Harry bumped into Frankie and now Bugs, who had let go of Joey's weight belt. For a brief moment panic ensued while they sorted themselves out. As soon as Bugs and Frankie got their headlamps in place they fell back in line and everyone finished in an uneventful manner.

Amy, standing on the bridge of the boat, was watching for the first sign of the Reverend coming back and at the same time praying to see bubbles from the scuba tanks indicating Harry and

Joey were coming up, hopefully with Bugs and Frankie. She couldn't wait to call the sisters and Paulo to tell them the good news. She also noticed Jimmy standing on deck looking out at the ocean. He looked sad. Why? Whenever Harry was around he looked this way. When he was alone with her or even alone with Harry he was funny and in great spirits. What made him so sad when Harry was nearby? Could Jimmy be jealous of her interest in Harry? But why? Jimmy was her good friend. She would tell him just that! But before she had a chance to talk to Jimmy the long awaited air bubbles came rolling up to the surface.

Harry breathed a sigh of relief when all heads and two Dolphins popped up next to the boat's ladder.

While the scuba group was getting on the boat Melody and Lindy spun around and did flips of joy.

You guys are fantastic. I can't thank you enough.

Happy to help! See ya, Jimmy, boy! Melody made a final leap before disappearing, with her friend, under the water.

Bugs and Frankie were helped out of their scuba gear and into the boat.

Amy rushed over to greet them. She gave Frankie, and then Bugs a big hug. "We are so happy to see both of you. I'm Amy Lafitte. That's Jimmy. We have a detective agency. Margaret and

Ray are my friends and our cover while we were looking for you on Castle Island. Harry and Joey are our friends and your rescue team. Bugs, your aunts sought our help in finding out what happened to you."

"I don't know how you found us but thank you!"

"The Dolphins played a big part in finding you. We'll tell you all about it later."

Amy heard chains rattling as the boat's anchor was lifted out of the water, pulled up and secured against the side of the boat. Joey started the engines and took off for the dock at the Marina Store. Since they were in a slow boat Amy figured the Reverend would be long gone before they even got there.

"Could I please call my brother?"

"Of course." Harry handed Frankie a cell phone while he talked to Bugs.

"In your case it was the money. It was all set up. He made you sign the papers for the sale of the island. He gave you the money and a drug that took effect once you were in your boat and leaving the island. You passed out, he followed you, boarded, took the money and blew up the boat. He put you in the cave through a secret door that has a passageway to the house. He probably had plans to sell Castle Island to a new buyer before he returned to his own country."

"I see. Wow! Thank you for finding us! What about Frankie?"

The phone at the Marina didn't answer. Frankie joined the conversation. "The Reverend offered me a job at the Castle. He brought me over here to be a chef. I understood enough of the language spoken by the staff to realize the Reverend was stealing jewelry and money from his guests. I told the Reverend that I wanted to go back to Key West right away. I think he figured I'd seen something I shouldn't have seen. He said he'd take me in the morning. That night he drugged my food and I ended up in here. That was six months ago."

Amy joined in. "The Reverend was ready to leave. The two week Pirate Fest gave him a reason to transport all the guests from the island to Key West. He put them up at the Blue Dolphin Hotel and then planned on making a run towards the Bahamas where he probably had a plane ready to take them back to his country with the stolen money and the stolen jewelry. I bet the guests at the Blue Dolphin are going to be in for a rude shock when they discover they are facing a big hotel bill when they paid the Reverend for their two week stay ahead of time. Frankie tried calling the Marina again. "No one is answering."

"Paulo could have just stepped out to help someone."

"I hope so. I'll try again in a few minutes."

Melody and Lindy headed for the Bahamas. Dolphin Rescue was having their once a month meeting and there's no place like the Bahamas to have a good time. Suddenly Melody stopped in the water, flipped around and headed back to Castle Island. She turned to Lindy at to the cave entrance. *Wait for me. I'll just be a second.* Melody headed into the dark cave opening under the water. Lindy, not being one who likes to wait, followed behind her.

CHAPTER NINE

The Rescue

As soon as they were in open sea SueAnn opened the door to the stateroom where Madame Sonya and Marta were tied up on the bed. The ladies were trussed expertly with their mouths taped making it hard to make any sounds. Their hands had been tied behind their backs with ropes connected to their feet. SueAnn returned to the cabin. "Ya did a good job." She called out to her friend who was at the wheel topside.

The Reverend realized these two women knew exactly what they were doing and were good at it, too. He had no doubt that any attempt on his part and SueAnn, or whatever name she was using, would have no trouble shooting him on the spot.

"Miss SueAnn, would you mind telling me your plans? I pray you have no intention of doing away with us."

They could hear Marta start to cry. SueAnn yelled. "Hey, can it, sister. Ya got a comfortable bed and I ain't thrown ya to the sharks...yet. Keep it up and I might."

The crying turned to a soft whimper. "Smart girl. She follows orders well. Ain't never fed sharks like that before but there's always a first and I just love first anything!"

That set Marta off again, this time louder than before.

She turned to the two men who were looking at her in horror. She wagged a finger at the Reverend. "Oh, see what you done, Rev! Ya got that child crying and all in an uproar. A famous actor once said 'Don't steal from people who can't afford it and don't kill people who don't deserve it!' Ya sure enough got the stealing part down. Thank ya, 'cause now I'm just gonna relieve ya of that stuff. Now, I ain't got no intention of doing away with anyone although ya make it a mighty tempting thought. If anyone deserves it, Rev...well I'm thinking about it. Here's a little heads up on the plans. I have someone picking me and Miranda up. Paulo, I know ya ain't connected to this band of thieves so before I get off this boat I'll untie ya." SueAnn laughed. "Now that's funny...after I get off this boat! More like this piece of junk. Really, Rev? Who paints their boat 'Hello Kitty' pink? And Miranda told me it don't go very fast. So listen up, before me and Miranda make our departure I'll tell ya where I hid the part to make the engines run. And I strongly suggest for ya health ya keep this pack of thieves tied up. They're a bad lot. Ya let 'em go and ya might end up going for a swim, minus the water wings, if ya get my drift. The Rev and his wife stole money from people who wanted to talk to their loved ones passed over. How awful is that, stealing from sad folks? And while Madame Sonya was busy with fake séances and phony Taro card readings the Rev, along with the band of hoodlums he called, The Staff, was stealing money and jewels from the rooms of his trusting guests. They was running a big business on other people's misfortunes. They didn't wanna get pinched by the cops so they planned on catchin' a ride out of here for the country they come from. Which sure as heck ain't here. I think maybe Romania. They is just a bunch of thieving gypsies. So me and Miranda plan on relieving them of the money and jewels they stole from them innocent people. I'd like to be a saint and give all the stuff back to them people he stole it from but what the heck, I never said I was a saint. So do as I say and nobody walks the plank. Know what I mean?"

SueAnn taped the Reverend's mouth. She pointed at Paulo. "I ain't taping your mouth shut but keep your trap closed or I will." She turned and headed topside to see what Miranda was doing. The girl could be a real flake sometimes.

Joey pulled up at the dock. He turned off the engines and threw the lines to Harry.

Amy turned to Bugs and Frankie. "Frankie, why don't you go surprise your brother? And Bugs I am sure your aunts are waiting to hear from you. Paulo has a phone in his store." The young couple took off.

Margaret and Ray followed them off the boat. "I think we've had enough excitement. We'll watch some of Pirate Fest, especially the Parade and then we're heading home. But if you need us for anything just call me. We have our car in a lot in town."

Amy was the first to hug them and say a quick goodbye. "Margaret, you have been a great friend. We can take it from here. I will talk to you back home."

Harry secured the boat and hauled the scuba gear onto the dock. He looked up and shaded his eyes with his hand. "Why are Bugs and Frankie coming back? And they're running."

"Something is wrong!" Frankie was in tears. My brother would never leave the store without a sign saying exactly when he would be back and he left his cash box open on the countertop. He'd never do that!

"Wait here." Amy ran towards the store.

Harry patted Frankie's arm. "Don't worry. I can hear the bands starting up. Do you think he just went to see the parade and he'll be back soon?

"No, I think something's wrong."

Amy put her hand on the door and asked to see what happened to Paulo. The mist swirled and then clear as day she saw Paulo and the Reverend walking toward the dock that had the gas tanks. She followed them to the dock and when she touched the gas

tank she saw them get on the Reverend's boat. She wasn't surprised

to see Lady Catherine pull out a gun and order the two men below

deck. She was a phony from the beginning.

She was dizzy for a second. Harry and Jimmy, Bugs and

Frankie all arrived together. Harry gently took her arm to steady her.

"What is it?"

"One Eye and Jocko told me Serena and Lafitte would be

here. I've got to find them. They're going to be at the pirate lookalike

contest. I've got to find Serena."

"Jimmy, I have to find Serena. Why don't you stay here with

Bugs and Frankie while I go look." She turned to Frankie. "Don't

worry Frankie, Paulo is somewhere downtown." It was just a little lie.

Frankie looked so panic Amy didn't want to tell her that her brother

had been kidnapped and was in a boat headed for somewhere she

didn't know yet. "And, Jimmy, do not call the police. That would be

silly. I'll find Paulo myself."

"Want me to help?" Frankie volunteered.

"No. If Paulo comes back, and you're in town, we'll never

get everyone together. Wait in the store."

"I know where he keeps a key."

"Good. Bugs, did you reach your aunts?"

"Yes. They're on the way over to the Marina right now. They said they can't wait to thank you."

"Harry, will you come with me?"

"All roads are blocked for cars but we can run. The town center is not far."

Looking around the Marina she realized the whole place looked totally deserted. The first time she was here there were people on boats sitting in lounge chairs, laughing with friends aboard, barbequing on small grills set up on the decks. Now nothing. Everyone was in town at the Pirate Fest.

As they ran Amy brought him up to date. "The Reverend took Paulo. When they got on his boat one of the guests, Lady Catherine, pulled out a gun and ordered both men below deck. I just bet Lady Catherine and her friend, Miranda, has all of them tied up. I knew there was something suspicious about those two! Miranda was at the wheel when the mist blotted out the vision. I'm not sure where they're heading. It could be Canada, the Bahamas or across the Gulf. But Serena would know."

In short time they were in downtown crowded with tourists and locals. Bands were warming up for the Parade, everyone was dressed in some manner of colorful pirate clothes whether it was a vest and pants or an ornate sash with a plastic saber across their chest.

Many men had eye patches. Some were drinking from pewter mugs, others from Pepsi bottles. Men, young and old, were in groups, hands on shoulders, singing pirate songs. She caught a glimpse of Blackbeard. Some of the pirates looked so authentic she wondered if they were the real thing because many were immortal thanks to Serena.

She was so busy looking around she stepped on a soda can. "Ow!" She slowed to a walk with a limp. "Now that was stupid. I should have been watching where I walk with all the partying going on."

Harry swept her up in his arms. "Point out Serena, ok?" "I can walk."

"If I put you down it will make that ankle worse. We can make better time like this."

Amy groaned. "Can't argue with logic."

Harry smiled back. "Good because I like carrying you. It's hard to find something to do for a woman who talks to Dolphins."

"Where is the pirate lookalike contest?"

"In front of Key West Cafe. We're almost there. You said something about mist and seeing everything that happened?"

"Okay, I think I better give you the quick version of who I am and who Serena is before we find her. I wanted to do this slowly but everything is happening too fast. So here goes! Serena is my Grandmother. She's a witch. A good witch. She sometimes gets a bit harsh but only if someone deserves it. My Grandad, is the real Jean Lafitte. Thanks to Serena he's an immortal. She is, too. I'm not. Not yet." In his arms Amy was close to his mouth which made her lose her train of thought. She closed her eyes in order to remember she had to tell him all the important things before he met Serena. "Serena gave me some powers, like silent talking to you, and talking to the Dolphins, also the power to touch something and go back in time and see what happened. When I touched the door at the Marina store, then the gas pump, I saw everything that happened to Paulo like it was a movie film. Serena gets around in a big black car that turns into a flying carriage which you might get a chance to see firsthand since I'm sure she will help us rescue Paulo. She hates bad people getting away with anything."

"Ok."

"I sure hope you believe me." She found herself fiddling with the button on his shirt. Concentrate, she told herself.

"You talk to Dolphins, see visions in the mist and can read my mind. I definitely believe you."

"There's more to tell you but there's no time right now." Amy pointed to a crowd of people. "There she is!" Amy waved frantically.

Marina called down the stairs to SueAnn, who had returned to her captive audience, regaling them with a rundown of her many exploits. "Hey, SueAnn, do ya think ya might take the wheel? I'd like to get some chow!"

"In a second!" She turned back to the Rev and Paulo. "So, Rev, ya didn't suspect me for a second, did ya?" She laughed and slapped her knee. "I might take up some of that movie acting sometime! I think I'm pretty good at it. Whaddya think?"

With his mouth taped all the Reverend could do was nod. Paulo didn't have the indignity of having his mouth taped but he knew better than to say a word.

"Thieves stealing from thieves! Something just darn right clever about that, ain't it? Bet it's in the Bible somewhere!"

"SueAnn!!" Miranda yelled.

"Hold ya horses, food addict. I said I'd be right there. Just a few more seconds." She turned to Paulo. "Now ya boys don't go anywhere or I'll have to get angry and ya don't want to see me angry, do ya?" She had an evil laugh.

They both nodded in panic at the thought.

SueAnn went topside to relieve Miranda at the wheel. "About time. I'm starving."

"Make something for me, too. Ok?"

"What exactly do ya do, Lady SueAnn?" Miranda stood there with her hands on her hips. "Seems to me I do everything."

SueAnn grabbed Miranda's shirt and pulled her close. "Don't ever try and cross me. I do plenty enough. And ya share of the haul will keep ya in that fancy wine and pate stuff that ya love so much. Not to mention lining ya current boyfriend's pockets." SueAnn snatched the hand gun out of her friend's hand and let her go. Miranda stumbled back. "Seeing as everything is under control from now on I'll keep the guns. About the loot...pass the suitcases to me right now. I want to see what we're gettin'."

"Yes, of course." Miranda stood there looking puzzled. She couldn't remember why SueAnn came topside.

"Something to eat? Remember? And the suitcases with the money and jewels. I swear ya got some kind of brain malfunction."

"Coming right up." Miranda disappeared below deck, happy to be away from SueAnn.

There was a time when she was her best friend. Not anymore. This was the last job she was going to pull with the older girl. She was going to collect her cut, find a house on a beach in the

Caribbean, and live a quiet life. She brought the luggage. SueAnn wasted no time going through their haul. "Now, Dawlin' this is what I call hittin' it big time!"

Harry put her down and Amy hobbled right into Serena's open arms. "My dear child, you look glowing."

At that moment Lafitte showed up carrying a large statue likeness of the pirate, Jean Lafitte. The statue was dressed in a black pirate shirt and black trousers, much like Lafitte was wearing right now. "Look what I won!"

Amy turned to Harry. "Serena, Lafitte, this is my friend, Harry Morgan. He took me to Castle Island in his boat and ---"

"---I know everything." She gave Harry a critical look.

Harry shook Lafitte's hand before the Pirate King was engulfed in admirers.

Serena gave Amy a once over.

"I tripped over a soda can."

Serena snapped her fingers. "Can't have the Pirate Queen hobbling around."

Suddenly the pain was gone. "I'm okay. Thanks ever so much!"

One Eyed and Jocko came running over. "Amy, are we glad to see you! You and Lafitte have ten minutes to get into costume and board the float. The parade is ready to start."

Amy whispered to Serena. "I have to rescue Paulo and arrest the Reverend and everyone on the Reverend's boat. I can't get on the float right now."

Serena whispered back. "I have everything taken care of. You and Lafitte get on the float. I'll take Harry with me. He knows what's going on."

"Yes, and I totally trust him."

"Then I do, too." Serena smiled. "Now you and Lafitte go show all these people a fun time."

Lafitte kissed Serena on her cheek. "Did you see Blackbeard? I can't believe he's here."

"I know." Serena shook her finger at him. "When you see him tell him not to light his beard on fire like he did at Mardi Gras. The Police don't care even if it is authentic!"

Lafitte laughed and took Amy's arm. "I'll tell him. But you know how he loves terrorizing people."

"Tell him I'll terrorize him if he does it here." Serena turned to Harry, "It's you and me to the rescue. Let's go."

I wish I could hear your voice. That kiss will have to wait.

You can hear me now! Serena gave you the power. Harry, I haven't had time to tell you everything.

I can't believe I can hear you like this! Listen, don't worry. Everything else can wait.

Harry smiled and followed behind Serena who was heading for a large boat tied up at the town dock.

They quickly boarded the fast boat and took off with Serena at the wheel. "Hold on!" Serena shouted. The moment they cleared the breakwater their boat turned into a flying pirate ship. He did not expect this at all.

"Everything okay, Harry?"

"Definitely okay. Great way to travel."

"We're on Blackbeard ship, the Queen Anne's Revenge. He loaned it to me."

"Wow!"

"Amy told me Blackbeard is in your family tree."

"Yes. I've always been fascinated by pirates."

"You're going to love our family."

Harry smiled. He did already.

"When we get back everyone will be talking about the airplane flying a pirate ship and also about the banner trailing off the stern."

Harry was amazed. "We're trailing a banner?"

"Of course. A flying pirate ship would look just too strange, especially if it's the Queen Anne's Revenge. Anyway they will all think it's a Pirate Fest advertising stunt."

"You are very smart."

"Why don't you call me Serena? They're heading across the Gulf."

"How do you know which way they went?

"One eye and Jocko were sitting on the roof of City Hall and they saw the Reverend's pink and white boat....who has a pink and white boat anyway? Anyway, the boys saw them speeding out of the Marina. That caught their attention. They told me right away. They said they watched the boat turn towards the Gulf at full speed."

"There are many inlets and islands off Florida. Maybe they are hiding somewhere."

"They're not. Watch this. Hold on!" Serena pulled on the wheel and the pirate ship rocketed straight up into thin air. "Harry, it's easier this way. I can track their trail from high up."

"Their trail?"

"There's always a trail. Most of the time it's ignored but if I want to find someone the path they are on lights up inside my crystal ball.

"I bet that comes in handy."

"It certainly does." Serena carefully took her crystal ball out of a padded case.

"I can spell you for a bit on the wheel." "Thank you, Harry."

Serena studied the glass globe. It changed into various colors. Harry watched, fascinated.

"Have you been watching over Amy?"

"Of course. I saw you when you sat next to her on the flight to Miami."

Harry smiled. "I bet you had a hand in the seating arrangements, too."

"What do you think? You weren't supposed to have anyone sitting next to you, right?"

"I like you!" He laughed.

Leaping up she looked over the side of the pirate ship. "I see them." Serena took the wheel. "We'll land a little behind them."

This time no one had to tell Harry to hang on. The pirate ship turned back into a fast boat when they landed on the water. Snapping her fingers she sent the pink and white boat into a major engine malfunction. Smoke billowed from the engines located below deck.

SueAnn and Miranda turned at the sound of the power boat behind them. They had no idea how a boat snuck up on them like that. Both women desperately looked for a gun, even a knife. They couldn't find any weapons. "What did ya do with ya gun?" SueAnn yelled over the roar of the power boat pulling up next to them.

"Miranda bristled. "Don't blame me. Everything has disappeared. And somethin' happened to this boat! The smoke is awful!"

Harry boarded their boat just as SueAnn rushed at him waving a chair leg. Miranda was right behind her with a wrench raised and aimed at his head.

Serena snapped her fingers and both women were stopped in mid-air, frozen in position.

Harry heard Paulo yelling in Spanish from below.

"Harry! I've never been so happy to see anyone in my life! Harry untied Paulo and they went above deck to hog tie and gag SueAnn and Miranda like they had done to their captives. They were going to be very uncomfortable when they came out of the trance Serena had put them in.

"Serena, this is Paulo, this is Amy's Grandmother."

"I am very happy to meet you! Thank you so much for rescuing me!"

"Start up the engine and take the boat back to the Marina." "But the engine blew up."

"Try again. I'm sure it's fixed."

Paulo turned over the engine and the boat purred. "How did the engine fix itself? How did you get here so fast? How did you find us?"

"So many questions!" Harry jumped over to the other boat. "We have a fast boat. Right Serena?"

"Right."

"That's how we got here so fast. Right now take this group to the town dock. I'll alert the Police so they can meet you there. Frankie is waiting for you at the Marina so go there after you turn over this group to the police."

"You found my sister?" Paulo was almost in tears.

"We did. Thanks to Amy."

"Wow! I thought she was kidnapped and taken out of the country. Where has she been?"

"Amy found Bugs and Frankie together. They were held captive in a cave under Ravensclaw. They had enough food and water. Frankie will tell you all about it."

"If they were in a cave under the house how did you get them out?"

"Joey and I went in there with scuba equipment."

"Frankie has never used scuba before!"

"I know but Bugs watched out for her."

"You're a good friend, Harry. How can I thank you?"

"I'll tell you what, one day make some of those homemade tamales for me."

"Definitely!"

Paulo watched as Harry boarded a boat he'd never seen before and when he turned he saw the fast boat take off. Amazingly the Reverend's boat was moving a lot faster than before. He could barely keep up with Harry. SueAnn and Miranda were thawing out! They didn't like the position of their hands tied to their feet and the gags that stifled their outcries of rage. Paulo couldn't hear what they were saying but by the flashing hatred in their eyes he figured it was something very bad. "Listen, ladies, calm down. After we turn you over to the police I'm sure you can vent all you want from a jail cell." Paulo laughed. He couldn't wait to see Frankie. His wife and two boys also loved her. After all these months not a day had gone by when he and his wife hadn't talked about finding Frankie. Not for one second did he ever think she was gone forever.

They made amazingly good time getting back to the town dock. Amy, the Police Chief Barker and Officer Boomer were waiting when they arrived. They quickly took the Reverend and his lot into custody along with SueAnn and Miranda. While the police were searching for the money and jewels the Reverend had stolen from his unknowing guests Amy removed the Reverend's gag.

"We rescued your house guests. Remember Bugs and Frankie?"

"How did you find them?"

"I had a lot of help from friends." Amy smiled. "Worry about yourself right now although where you and your clan are going you'll make a lot of new friends. Maybe you can con them with your fake séances. Probably not but you'll have a lot of time to try."

"What about the bird watching?"

"We'd rather spend our time catching crooks like you."

Chief Barker called from above deck. "We found it all. Money, jewels, everything and one more thing...a bag with gold dust and a gold coin."

"I'll take that." Amy put it in her pocket. "It belongs to a friend of mine."

The haul also included all the luggage and the clutch bag that held Lady Catherine aka SueAnn's ruby and diamond necklace, ring, bracelet and tiara that was no doubt lifted from someone who didn't know who had stolen their magnificent family jewels.

Chief Barker stomped down the stairs and urged SueAnn, Miranda, the Reverend and his wife to go topside to join his staff who had been arrested at the Blue Dolphin Hotel. Three deputies got the group into the Key West Jail Wagon and drove off.

Amy watched them go before turning to the Police Chief. "Maybe I'll see you next year."

"I certainly hope so and maybe you'll bring that flying pirate ship with you. It was great advertising."

"So we heard but we didn't have anything to do with that. We do have a fast boat that we'll be leaving in a little later." Amy was the picture of innocence.

Chief Barker laughed. "Next time file a flight plan!" A cruiser pulled up and he got in.

The day was bright and the Pirate Fest was just starting.

On their way back to the Marina Amy introduced Serena, now joined by Lafitte, to Paulo, who said his hello's and then took off running when he saw Frankie. "Serena, where is my Mom and Dad?" Amy looked around.

"When you and Jimmy left for Miami your Mom and Dad decided to take a little honeymoon in London, where you were born. They plan on staying for a while."

"It's probably been hard on them."

"Harder on you, my precious child."

"I know, thank you." Amy hugged Serena. She was sorry her Mom and Dad weren't here but in a way some didn't miss them that much. She loved Serene more than anyone.

Harry was as happy to see Amy as she was to see him. *Miss Detective, do you think we'll ever have any moments alone?*

I think that can be arranged.

You're Pirate Amy now. I bet they want you to ride the float next year.

That was the first thing Jocko said when the parade ended. I knew it. You made a beautiful Pirate Queen.

Harry, how did you know?"

Serena had a special TV viewing for us on the way back!

Amy laughed and waved at Serena who wandered off with Lafitte.

"We'll see you later." Serena called back to Amy.

I see One Eye and Jocko headed this way. Harry brought his two pirate friends up to date on everything that had happened.

Paulo hugged Amy again. How could he possibly thank her from bringing back his beloved sister? Turning to his wife and his two sons by his side, Paulo couldn't stop crying and hugging Frankie.

At one point he whispered in Frankie's ear. "I can't believe the police haven't asked for your papers!"

Frankie whispered back, "I'm going to be legal here. Bugs and I fell in love. We're getting married as soon as possible."

Paulo turned to the group that had gathered and announced, "I have more wonderful news! My dear sister Frankie and Bugs Robichaux are getting married! My family welcomes Bugs!"

Bugs, who was now being smothered with love by his two aunts, Lynne and Gayle who had just arrived, smiled and brought the two families together.

The sisters thanked Amy and Jimmy from their hearts. "Also Harry and his friend, Joey who is not here, went into the cave with scuba gear and brought Bugs and Frankie out safely." It was Harry's turn to be adored by the aunts.

Even with all the noise going on, the crowd was suddenly aware of seven dolphins flipping and dancing in the water near them. Melody rested her chin on a step above the water.

Amy, Amy, you told me about the pirate treasure map. We found it! We found it!

You found the map?

No, silly Billy, we found the treasure!

What? Where? I can't believe it!

It was near the beach area in the cave. When we went in to get the kids I saw the glitter of gold so I called for reinforcements. Dolphin Rescue at your service. That beach must have been a small cliff at one time but the tide wore it away. Pirates must have dug it into the cliff side, but the years broke down the wooden chest and spilled the jewels and gold pieces all around. Here are some.

Melody leaped high out of the water and spit out rubies, emeralds and gold coins that landed at Amy's feet.

A huge gasp went up from the crowd.

"Bugs, the Dolphins found the pirate treasure on your island."

Amy stood there transfixed as one after another the Dolphins sent jewels and gold coins raining down onto the dock.

There's a lot more where this came from. Thank you, my friends!

"There's a lot more of this treasure, too."

The sisters looked at Bugs. "That will be our wedding gift to you and Frankie, my dear."

Bugs hugged one aunt then the other. "You mean that? Now I don't have to sell the island. Frankie and I will make Ravensclaw a successful Bed & Breakfast!" Bugs took Frankie's hand. "When we were in the cave Frankie and I used to talk about the island and what we could have done with it. We guessed, but we weren't positive, that Ravensclaw was right above us the whole time but we had no way of escape. In the beginning I tried to swim out but the exit was underwater and I went as far as I could, holding my breath, but there was no end in sight. That idea didn't work."

The aunts gestured to Frankie to come close. They hugged her and whispered, "We are so happy. You are a lovely young girl. You took care of each other during all those months. That makes a very lasting bond. We are happy to welcome you into our family."

The aunts turned to Bugs and finished each other's sentences. "I hope you and Frankie will have a place for us when we come to visit. Maybe you might even have Murder Mystery Dinner Parties. We love those parties so much!"

"Oh, you bet! In fact we need some ideas for the plots! Do you have some in mind?"

"Do we ever!" Gayle laughed. "Lynne has always wanted to write those things...but only if you like them."

"We will love them. This is like a dream come true. I never imagined an ending like this."

"Bugs, we knew we'd find you." The aunts were so happy they were in tears.

"I was six years old and Mom and Dad died. You took me in as your own."

"You father was our only brother. When you came to us you became our son and now we will have a daughter, too. You don't know how happy that makes us. Your Mom and Dad would have been so proud this day."

They all turned to see the Police Chief headed their way.

Chief Barker approached the group followed by Officer Boomer.

One Eye and Jocko waved goodbye and headed back to the festival going on Downtown. They planned on checking in with Harry later to hear what happened.

Much to the surprise of everyone who knew about Frankie's immigration status in Florida, Chief Barker didn't mention it.

Amy did a quick introduction of everyone Chief Barker hadn't met.

The Police Chief pulled out a small notebook with a list of names. "The Reverend, whose real name is Damian Voltic and his wife Sadie, didn't say a word. But in the world of con artists they rank at the top. Marta, who was not related to the Voltic family, was very helpful. We also rounded up Voltic's staff, consisting of his three daughters who were his staff on the island, and two daughters

who were part of the permanent housekeeping staff at the Blue
Dolphin Hotel. She no doubt directed many guests to Ravensclaw.
Apparently Bug's Uncle Clyde, who left him the island, was very ill,
but believed Damian was honest and had made Ravensclaw a place
for spiritual healing. Damian Voltic stole from most of his guests but
in a way they couldn't say exactly who had stolen from them. Many
of the guests, being wealthy, absorbed the losses and kept quiet.
Especially the single women who didn't want any trouble to come
after them if they had spoken up. Marta told us everything. Voltic
planned on leaving during the night, taking not only his family but
the money and jewels he had stolen during his time at Ravensclaw.
His plans were made a bit complicated when SueAnn, AKA Lady
Catherine, and Miranda refused to stay at the Blue Dolphin Hotel.
They had their own plans to kidnap the Reverend and do away with
the Voltic family and all the while he was planning the same fate for
them. The ladies kidnapped the Voltic's at the Marina, took over the
boat, and headed for the bayou in Louisiana." Chief Barker had a
surprised look on his face. "Thieves stealing from thieves. I've never
run into this before. Incredible. They told Paulo, who was innocent of
any wrong doing, that they were going to release him. They're all in
the Key West jail."

"Chief Barker, thank you!" The two aunts were beaming with happiness and relief at finding Bugs.

"It's my job." The Chief smiled and tipped his Navy blue baseball cap with its signature Key West Police logo. By the way, Pirate Amy, you made a very beautiful Pirate Queen. And your Dad looks amazingly like Jean Lafitte."

Serena spoke up. "He gets that all the time."

Everyone was smiling. It was a great day.

Chief Barker started to leave but turned back.

"Congratulations are in order. Bugs, I heard you and Frankie are getting married!"

"How did you know?" Amy was amazed.

"We have powers, too. Bye all!" Chief Barker grinned. Then he and Officer Boomer turned and walked away, leaving the group amazed.

Everyone but Serena.

Jimmy walked up behind Amy and wiped the sweat off his brow. "Wow! This has been some day!"

Amy started laughing. "Where have you been all this time?"

"I knew everything was going to work out so I was over at Trader Mike eating oysters and telling tall tales."

"I think it's time to go home."

"Aww. And just when things were getting interesting."

"Jimmy, I think this is just the beginning." Amy slipped the bag of gold dust and the gold coin into his hand. It was the first time she saw tears come to Jimmy's eyes. He knew in that moment she would always be his best friend.

CHAPTER TEN

Going Home

After a thousand goodbyes the aunts, Lynne and Gayle, with Bugs, went over to Paulo's apartment, over the Marina Store, to celebrate the return of their nephew and his engagement to Paulo's sister, Frankie.

Serena, Lafitte and Amy, along with Jimmy and Harry, spent the rest of the day at Pirate Fest, ending with a late night supper at Trader Mike's place.

"These Oyster Po'boys are really good. Almost as good as the ones at The Acme House in the French Quarter."

"The secret is in the bread." Jimmy prided himself on his knowledge.

Amy smiled. She had seen the same sign Jimmy had. "Jimmy, Trader Mike has a big sign over the bar saying he gets the bread for his Po'boys from Leidenheimer's bakery in New Orleans. Everyone knows it wouldn't be a Po'boy without Leidenheimer's bread."

Jimmy laughed. "Amy Lafitte, you're a good witch in the making."

Amy looked at Serena and smiled. "That I am."

"Okay, everyone, time to go home." Serena stood.

Harry walked out with the group wondering when he'd see Amy again.

"Harry, you come with us." Serena stated.

"I got a call last night. I have to go to Houston. I delivered the plane to a buyer but now I have to give him some flying lessons. His business is at the Port. He flies float planes to the rigs.

"Well that settles it. You'll never get a flight out of Key West anyway. We can make a slight detour and drop you off at the Port. I'm sure you can make arrangements to come through New Orleans on your way back to Miami."

"I would love to."

Serena took his arm as they walked out of the restaurant. "My Granddaughter told me you're related to Blackbeard."

"I am."

"I'll make sure when you're in New Orleans we invite him over to dinner."

"The real one?" Harry surprised himself asking such as outrageous question. He smiled.

"Of course! We just have to keep him from setting his beard on fire. He absolutely loves to do that and it always causes a mad stampede out the front door by guests who didn't know he's such a rascal."

Amy was walking with Jimmy. She was delighted Harry and Serena were getting on so well. If she said anything she might spoil it so she just kept very quiet.

It was a short walk from Trader Mike's to the town dock. They all boarded the fast boat Serena and Harry had been in earlier. As soon as they cleared the breakwater, and were out of the harbor, the boat turned into a flying pirate ship once again.

Lafitte stood at the wheel laughing and ordering everyone about.

Serena whispered to Harry. "Lafitte feels right at home. This is his ship, you know."

"You mean his original ship?" When, he wondered, was he going to stop asking stupid questions. Totally amazed is a mild world for what he was experiencing.

"Of course."

Amy walked up and Serena sighed, leaving the two alone. "I am happy you get along so well with Serena."

"I hope so but I keep asking stupid questions. Amy, you have an incredible family."

"There are no stupid questions. Only stupid answers. One day when we have some time alone I'll tell you the whole remarkable story about what happened to me."

"I would love to spend time alone with you, a lot of time."

"Me, too. When you finish in Houston I hope you stop in New Orleans on your way back home."

"I've was just invited to dinner. And I really like Serena."

"Serena likes you. I'm looking forward to showing you the Quarter. It's a magical place. There is so much to show you about my world."

"We had a great time tracking down the Reverend. I've never met anyone like Serena. Do you know she knew I was related to Blackbeard?"

"Of course. Serena knows everything. There are no secrets in this family. Blackbeard came over a lot during Mardi Gras. He's an immortal like just about all my family. Except me." Amy looked over the side. "Look, we're flying over an oil rig!"

Men standing on the deck of the oil rig were pointing up in the night sky. She wondered if they were thinking that seeing a flying pirate ship was just the result of drinking too much whiskey.

"I want to know all about you."

"And I want to tell you. Serena told me my Mom and Dad are in Europe and probably not coming back."

"Why?"

"I don't know, but it's okay. I spent thirteen years in that orphanage Jimmy talked about. When we were all reunited in New Orleans I felt disconnected from them."

"I can understand that. People change."

"Maybe with time, things might change again. I don't know. Serena means everything to me now."

"My Mom died when I was young. After a while I couldn't remember what she looked like. Things do change."

"I was very reluctant to talk to you about my past when we first met. It takes me time to trust anyone."

"Amy, you and I are so much alike. I've never felt like I could bare my soul to anyone until now."

Amy didn't know what to say. She was overwhelmed with feelings. Harry understood. He was, too. Sometimes you just don't need to say anything.

They arrived in Houston all too soon. Lafitte guided the pirate ship down to a water landing which terrified a boat of sport fishermen who pulled anchor and raced out of there.

With everyone looking on, Amy felt like the center of attention. Harry gave her a big hug and whispered. "I want more than anything to give you a kiss but Serena is watching me very closely! But I'll definitely see you soon."

Amy smiled.

Harry spent the next few minutes thinking about Amy and saying goodbye to everyone. Climbing into a small boat, with a single engine, he headed in the direction of a fleet of float planes belonging to the buyer who was waiting for him.

I can't wait to get back. This is going to be the fastest flying lesson I've ever given!

I can hear you, Harry.

I'm crazy about you!

Me, too! See you soon.

"You're not going to cry, are you?"

Amy turned to see Jimmy looking up at her with a sad look on his face. "Ah, Jimmy, me darlin', maybe I will, but not so's I'm seen by anyone."

"I understand."

"Do ya now?" Amy ruffled his red hair. She knew he would grumble and rush to smooth it down, which it only stayed for a little while, before springing up in the back again.

"I got a phone call from Milly. She said Kathy, remember her, she was at the Devereux Plantation when you fell off the ladder."

"Yes, the nurse."

"That's the one. Well a friend of hers came to visit and they went to Serena's new Ponchatrian Beach last night---"

"---I didn't know it was up and running."

"Things have been a bit busy lately. There hasn't been a moment to tell you. Anyway Kathy and her friend went into the Haunted House of Mirrors only her friend didn't come out."

"What do you mean she didn't come out?"

"Geez, Amy....she disappeared!"

"Oh, no! Does Serena know?"

"One of Lafitte's pirate buddies has been running the place and he just called her a few minutes ago. He wanted to make sure Kathy's friend didn't just run off with one of the carny guys so he waited until now before he called."

"What did Kathy say?"

"She hired us to find her friend."

"I have a million questions." Amy started thinking about the new case at once.

"Kathy's a nervous wreck. Milly said Kathy's been back and forth to the office." Jimmy bumped into Amy as Serena turned the pirate ship around faster than any ship had ever turned before. In just

seconds they were flying warp speed back to New Orleans.

Made in the USA
Middletown, DE
29 May 2025

76184362R00159